THE Christmas
MAIL-ORDER BRIDE

KIT MORGAN
BESTSELLING AUTHOR

ANGEL CREEK PRESS

The Christmas Mail-Order Bride (Holiday Mail-Order Brides, Book One) by Kit Morgan

© 2014 2nd Edition Kit Morgan
1st Edition published 2013 by Kit Morgan

Cover Design and Interior format by The Killion Group
http://thekilliongroupinc.com

License Notes

DEDICATION

To Mary Tackett, whom I affectionately referred to as Gran Ma Mere, and whom I kept knee-deep in romance novels for the last two years of her glorious ninety-three-year life. Unfortunately, she could read them faster than I could supply them! Her daughter Gayle and I had to stay on our toes to keep up with her voracious reading habit!

I had the pleasure of creating a small token book for Mary (okay, so it started out as a birthday card Gayle and I were making and turned into a book!) that told the tale of her life as a young wife and mother raising her nine children on an apple farm in the Lake Chelan area of Washington state. Within its pages, one quickly learns that the Tackett family is a fun-loving, life-living bunch. They have been a great source of joy since the day I met them and I am honored by their friendship. So here's to the hard-working Tacketts, who by simply breathing the air in apple country can tell you what apple is growing in what orchard and then some! Love you guys!

OTHER TITLES IN THIS SERIES INCLUDE:

A Mid-Summer's Mail-Order Bride
(Holiday Mail-Order Brides, Book Twelve)

For other books by Kit Morgan visit her website
at **www.authorkitmorgan.com**

ONE

New Orleans, October 1870

Summer James sat outside Mrs. Ridgley's office and listened in horror to the conversation going on inside. Though the door was closed, she could still make out the bulk of the argument as Mrs. Ridgley and someone called Slade battled it out. She had no idea why they would be arguing about her, but she'd caught enough to conclude that that was exactly what they were doing.

Summer had arrived with a letter of recommendation written by Mrs. Teeters, the head of the Winslow Orphanage. Once she turned eighteen, she had been given a choice: find respectable work in New Orleans, or find it elsewhere. "Elsewhere," in this case, meant becoming a mail-order bride to some far-off settler or farmer thousands of miles away. As she hadn't been able to find any sort of decent work in the Crescent City – not a great surprise, as the city was only five years removed from the American War Between the States – she was forced to pursue what opportunities lay in the "elsewhere" category.

She jumped as Slade slammed a fist down on Mrs. Ridgley's desk. Would he harm the woman? What could he possibly be so upset about?

Just as she made up her mind to enter unannounced and interrupt the heated argument for the sake of Mrs. Ridgley's safety, two huge Negro men came storming up the stairs from the first floor of the building and did the interrupting for her. "Get this vile man out of my sight!" Mrs. Ridgley ordered as they burst into the room.

"You haven't seen the last of me, Eugena! You can't keep putting me off forever!" the man called Slade spat. Summer could see into the office, and shrank a little in her chair. He was tall and lean and had an ugly scar running down the left side of his face.

He glared at the two men, who had planted themselves one on each side of Mrs. Ridgley's desk, and snarled. One of the men raised an amused brow as if to say *oh, really?* then pointed to the door and took a threatening step forward.

"Indeed, Jethro – please see Mr. Slade out. *All* the way out," Mrs. Ridgley stated firmly.

"With pleasure, ma'am!" said Jethro, who now closed the distance to Mr. Slade.

Summer quickly glanced toward the stairs and fought the urge to bolt in their direction as Mr. Slade stormed out of the office just ahead of the bigger man. He stopped right in front of her and glared, his eyes narrowed to slits. She didn't deem herself a great beauty – she was underweight, her blue eyes had dark circles under them from lack of sleep, and her long blonde hair needed a good washing. Yet the man looked her over like she was some prized piece of expensive horseflesh before he licked his upper lip and smiled. He quickly bent to her and whispered, "I'll see you later, sweet."

But before she could so much as blink an eye, he was yanked upright by Jethro, who hauled him to the stairs and none too gently began to shove him down the stairwell.

Summer gulped back her fear and chanced a peek at Mrs. Ridgley, who now stood behind her desk, a firm look of resolve on her face, and motioned the other man to bend down so she could whisper in his ear.

When she was done giving him instructions, he smiled and strolled out of the office to Summer. "Mrs. Ridgley will see you now, miss," he told her in a deep, pleasant voice.

"Th-thank you," she said as she gripped her reticule and stiffly stood. A chill went up her spine at the odd snippets she'd overheard of Mrs. Ridgley and Mr. Slade's argument. Did she dare ask what it was about? From what she could make out, it almost sounded like Mr. Slade was trying to *buy* her!

"Please sit down, dear. Solomon, stay outside the office until Miss James is ready to depart, will you? Then I want you to escort her back to Winslow."

"It would be my pleasure, Mrs. Ridgley." He smiled warmly before he turned to Summer.

"Whenever you're ready to leave, Miss James, I'll be right here."

Summer could only give a solitary nod in return as he backed out of the office and closed the door behind him.

"Please, sit down," Mrs. Ridgley told her.

Summer sent her a weak smile and sat in an old chair in front of an equally old desk. In fact, the desk and chairs weren't the only things in Mrs. Ridgley's office that looked worn out. The rest of the furniture had also seen better days, and she noticed how the wallpaper was peeling in several places. But the office as a whole was clean and orderly, the windows and their curtains clean though frayed.

She briefly wondered if being there was such a good idea, and sent up a quick prayer that the state of Mrs. Ridgley's office wasn't an indication of the people who utilized her mail-order bride service. Then, wasn't she in a similar state – poor-looking, feeling worn out, frayed, and with no place left to go? At least she was clean.

"I've searched my files and picked the applicant I think most suits you."

"Applicant? I thought I would get to choose between several."

Mrs. Ridgley's face fell, and she clasped her hands in front of her on the desk. "The truth is, Miss James, I'm afraid we've only had one suitable gentlemen answer our advertisement so far. Of course you're welcome to wait until we receive more, but I wouldn't advise it."

Disappointment sunk hard and fast into

Summer's belly; her insides knotted up with pain. "But what if ... what if I don't care for the gentleman?"

Mrs. Ridgley sighed heavily. "Miss James, the alternative you face is nothing I would wish upon anyone. I strongly advise you to take what we have to offer."

Summer felt her feet go suddenly cold, as if her blood had ceased to flow through her veins, her very heart stopped by Mrs. Ridgley's words. "Alternative?"

"Miss James," Mrs. Ridgley began, her voice stern. "Take this offer of marriage from..." She quickly looked at the papers in front of her. "... this Mr. Clayton Riley. He sounds like a wonderful man – and look, he even sent his picture." She slid a small photograph toward her.

Summer picked it up to get a better look. It was cracked and faded – she could hardly tell what the man looked like! She turned it over to see if anything had been written on the back. Good heavens, was that *blood*?

"He has already sent train and stage fare ..."

"What?!"

"It's something we ask for up front so we can get a bride out of ... sorry, out *to* their prospective groom right away, anxious as most gentleman are to get married." Mrs. Ridgley gave her an imploring look at that point.

Slowly, Summer began to put it all together. "What did that man ... Mr. Slade ... want with me?"

Mrs. Ridgley closed her eyes for a moment.

"Mr. Slade is a very bad man, Miss James. He's been a thorn in my side ever since the war ended and I started this business."

"But what did he want with me?"

The woman swallowed hard and looked at her. "We were business associates at one time, but I left after the war to do other things. More worthwhile things, such as helping young ladies as yourself find a better life than the one offered here."

Summer gripped her reticule and stared Mrs. Ridgley down. "What sort of business were you in?"

"I do not wish to discuss that. Ever. Now, if you would read over the gentleman's application, we can proceed."

A tear came to Summer's eye. She could hazard a guess what that had been about, and understood what would happen if she turned down the one applicant Mrs. Ridgley's mail-order bride service managed to get. Clearly Mrs. Ridgley was dealing with the unwanted, the women no other mail-order bride service would touch. After all, who wanted a dirty little orphan like herself with no idea of how to be a lady? Or a starving widow left alone because of the brutality of war? Or perhaps even a "soiled dove" desperate for a better life?

Of course, men like Mr. Slade did. She'd heard rumors of how certain disreputables preyed upon them night and day – went hunting for them, in fact, like a spider seeking its next meal. When a woman came within range, they grabbed her up and imprisoned her in their web of deceit and lies, indebting the victim to them so deeply there was no escape.

So Mr. Slade *had* been trying to buy her! Well, perhaps *buy* wasn't the right word –*claim* might be better.

And that was the choice she faced. If she didn't take Mr. Riley's offer of marriage, what was she to do? Continue to wander the streets until she found a job? There was no time – in two days she had to be out of Winslow, and she had nowhere else to go. People had already complained to the law about Winslow's overcrowded walls. No wonder Mr. Slade told her he'd see her later – he likely intended to snatch her up as soon as she left them! "Oh, no … what am I to do?"

Mrs. Ridgley shoved the papers across the desk, took a pen, dipped it in an inkwell, and held it out to her. "Sign this, and I guarantee you'll survive, far away from Mr. Slade and his ilk. If you don't, I know what awaits you. They'll make a slave of you, Miss James, and there's nowhere you can run from men like that."

A lone tear streamed down Summer's cheek as she put forth a shaky hand and took the pen. Her lower lip trembling, she scrawled her signature across several pages, then set the pen down.

Mrs. Ridgley breathed a sigh of relief. "I'll have Solomon escort you back to Winslow. He'll return in two days to fetch you to the train station. Do not leave the orphanage until he comes, do you understand?"

Summer nodded, took a handkerchief from her reticule and wiped her tear away. "What ... what sort of man is this Mr. Riley?" she sputtered, then blew her nose.

Mrs. Ridgley picked up the papers and leafed through them. "From what I can discern, he seems like a kind, gentle man. He was a captain in the Union army, and is now a sheriff in a small town out west."

"Out west? How far out west? Where are you sending me?" Summer asked, her eyes wide.

Mrs. Ridgley leafed through the papers once again before she looked at her across the desk. "I'm sending you to ... Nowhere."

Summer blinked, stunned. "Nowhere?"

"I should explain. 'Nowhere,' in this case, is the name of a town in the Washington Territory. You'll take the train as far as Salt Lake, then the stage for the remainder of the journey."

Summer's mouth dropped open in shock. How utterly fitting! She could just imagine introducing herself a couple of months from now. *Hello, I'm Summer Riley and I'm from Nowhere.*

She wanted to bury her face in her hands, but didn't for Mrs. Ridgley's sake. The woman was trying to save her from a fate far worse than the western frontier. Mr. Slade was obviously seeking women for his ... *business*, and had no qualms about stealing one such as herself right off the streets! Mrs. Ridgley was right – it was only a matter of time before he got his hands on her.

She straightened in her chair. "Thank you."

Mrs. Ridgley smiled. "If I can help you, or any other girl, get a chance at a better life, then I've done my job. No matter if you're an orphan, widow, or anything else."

Summer managed a smile. "Again, thank you. There are others coming of age at Winslow. They'll need a chance too if unable to make it by themselves."

"I already know. Mrs. Teeters has given me a list of names."

"She has?"

Mrs. Ridgley smiled. "My dear sweet girl, your name was at the top of the list."

Summer smiled and nodded. "Mrs. Teeters … I'll miss her terribly. She knows where I'm going then?"

"Yes, dear. She knows. And I've also told her that the man who awaits you is a kind man, a gentle man, just as his letter here states."

"It's a relief to know." Summer stood, took a deep breath and turned to the door. She stared at it a moment before she squared her shoulders and closed her eyes in resignation. In a matter of weeks she would start a new life as Mrs. Clayton Riley from Nowhere. She just hoped this Mr. Riley was as gentle and kind as Mrs. Ridgley said.

Nowhere, Washington Territory, November 1870

Clayton Riley quickly pulled back his fist and swung. "You did *what?*"

His brother Spencer reeled from the blow, landed on the desk behind him and rolled off it onto the floor. He quickly scrambled to his feet and held up both hands in front of him. "I thought it would do you good!" he argued.

"How could you do such a thing?" Clayton yelled. "Are you plumb out of your mind? Get your sorry hide over here so I can hit you again!"

Spencer was smart enough to keep his distance at this point, especially when he unexpectedly laughed. That wasn't going to help the situation, but dagnabit, the situation in question *was* funny!

"I can't believe you would do this to me! Of all the low down, idiotic ..." Clayton lamented as he began to chase his younger brother around the only desk in the sheriff's office. Their one prisoner watched from his cell and chuckled as one brother, on one side of the desk, bobbed and weaved to dodge the fists of the one on the other side.

"This is getting you nowhere. Clayton, you might as well face the music and get hitched!"

Clayton's eyes narrowed to dark, green slits. He loved his brother, really and truly he did, but right now he wanted to kill him. "Get hitched? Get *hitched*? I'm not the one that sent away for a mail-order bride, *you* did!"

"With your best interest in mind, and because I love you! What else am I supposed to do? Ma thinks you ought to get married first, not me!

And you wouldn't want to break our mother's li'l ol' heart now, would you? Besides, I thought it would make a perfect Christmas present!"

"Christmas present? It's not even Thanksgiving yet! Besides, when you asked me what I wanted for Christmas, I told you I needed a new pair of boots!"

"But isn't a bride so much better?"

Clayton lunged across the desk. "I'm going to kill you now," he said evenly.

"But Clayton, you can't!" Spencer chortled as he jumped out of range.

"And why not?" Clayton said through clenched teeth.

"Because the stage is pulling up at this very moment – and she's on it!"

Clayton's mouth dropped open in shock.

Their prisoner took one look at him and burst into riotous laughter. Clayton, his mouth still hanging open, slowly turned and glared at him. The drunken cowboy laughed even louder.

With lightning speed Clayton drew his gun and pointed it at the cell.

The cowboy immediately pressed his lips together and raised both hands in the air. It was all he could do to stop the several snorts of amusement that still managed to escape.

Clayton snarled, turned, and aimed his gun at Spencer instead as the sound of the stage reached his ears.

Spencer casually looked at the door behind him, then the gun in Clayton's hand. "I bet she's pretty."

"I don't care what she looks like. Get out

there and fix this."

"She's expecting to meet and marry one Clayton Riley, not his poor nothing of a little brother Spencer! You can't disappoint her!"

"Watch me."

"But, Clayton, think of Ma! She'll be so upset!"

"How can she be upset? Don't tell me she knows about this too?"

Spencer flashed a brilliant smile. "Whose idea do you think it was?"

Clayton groaned, went to rub his forehead, and accidentally hit himself with the butt of his gun.

The cowboy in the cell, unable to hold it together any longer, fell into complete and utter hysterics once again.

Clayton wheeled on him, but it didn't do a lick of good. The man was now doubled over and gulping air as tears formed in his eyes.

Clayton growled low in his throat and again faced his brother. "Fix this, Spencer – or I'm sending you to Uncle Harlan in Clear Creek. You can be *his* deputy, and I'll tell Ma she's just going to have to get along without her baby boy."

Spencer's amused face suddenly sobered. "Clear Creek? Oh no! I'm not dealing with that bunch of loons! They're plumb loco in that town! No, I'm afraid you'll just have to get hitched – and then everyone will be happy!"

Clayton began to suck air through his nose. His face red, he took a deep breath and yelled, "Get. Out. There. Now!"

Spencer's brow puckered. "So pushy. All right, I'll take care of it. Just don't be so angry. Ma and I really do have your best interest in mind. You're the one that's been sulking around town since last winter like a lonely coyote."

"I have not been sulking."

"You've been cranky, too."

"Spencer!"

"They say lonely people die young…," came from behind him.

"Rufus, have you decided you're not in enough trouble already?"

"I'm just sayin' …"

Spencer used the distraction the prisoner provided to inch to the door. He put his hand on the knob and began to open it. "All right, but if she's pretty, I bet you'll have a hard time sending her back!"

"Highly unlike–" Clayton never finished his sentence. His jaw dropped like a falling brick, his eyes grew round as saucers, and for the first time in his career as a lawman, he lost his grip on his gun.

It hit the floor, and fired.

The young woman in the doorway screamed in pain and dropped to the floor.

"Good God!" Clayton heard himself cry. He scrambled around the desk and ran to the woman as she writhed in pain on the threshold and clutched her foot. "Ma'am! Ma'am, are you all right?"

"Of course she's not all right," Spencer snapped. "You just *shot* her."

"Spencer!" Clayton barked.

"Well, I was just pointing out the obvious!"

"Spencer, for God's sake get out of here and fetch Doc!"

"All right, all right!" he said, then quickly bent to the pretty (and injured) woman in the doorway. "I'm Spencer Riley – I'm going to be your new brother-in-law!" he blurted before he jumped up, hurried past her, and ran down the street.

A crowd began to gather on the boardwalk outside. Clayton ignored them as he scooped the woman into his arms, slammed the door shut with his foot, and carried her to the desk where he very gently sat her down. "I'm so sorry this happened. Here, let me take a look at it."

Tears streamed down her face as she gritted her teeth against the pain. "I ... I ...," she stammered, just before her eyes rolled back in her head and she toppled over.

Clayton grabbed her before she fell off the desk and held her to him.

"She done fainted," Rufus stated matter-of-factly from the cell.

"I can see that. Now shut up."

"She sure is pretty ..."

"Rufus!" Clayton warned.

Rufus finally took the hint and stayed silent.

But when Clayton looked down at the woman cradled in his arms, he could see it was true – she *was* pretty. Beautiful in fact, so much so that she took his breath away. Of course, knowing he'd just accidently shot her did too, and as he stared at her unconscious form he heard his brother's words echo in his mind. *If she's pretty, I bet you'll have a hard time sending her back ...*

A brutal blast of loneliness hit him at that moment. The emptiness in his heart screamed for recognition as he held the woman and waited for her to regain consciousness – or for Doc to get there, whichever came first. Just so long as one or the other happened soon ... like, that very instant!

He looked longingly at the door. "C'mon, Doc. Don't leave me here like this." If he held her any longer, he was going to start listening to his heart. And that was something he didn't want to have happen ever again.

TWO

Summer forced her eyes open. She'd lost consciousness – of that she was sure – and now fought to keep her wits about her. How could this happen? What would Mr. Riley think of her now? Injured no sooner than she got off the stage! But who shot her? The man who carried her into the sheriff's office? Was *he* Clayton Riley?

Oh, good Lord! If he was, then they certainly hadn't got off on the right foot! *Oh dear …* make that the left, as that's the foot he shot.

He had her crushed against his broad chest, and she managed to look up at him just as someone yelled out, "Got it!" She tried to turn her head, but he held her so firmly against him she couldn't move. She weakly flayed an arm about to get his attention.

"Jumpin' johnnies! She's lucky it's just a flesh wound!" a creaky voice cried.

The man who'd plastered her against his chest pushed himself away a few inches, just enough for her to look up at him. A small whimper slipped out at what she saw. His hair was thick and dark, his jaw square and strong.

He gazed at her with two dark green eyes that could have been emeralds.

She whimpered again, not at the man's striking looks, but at the horrible pain in her left foot.

"It's okay, ma'am. Doc here just got the bullet out and is gonna fix you up. Hang on now, can ya do that for me?"

Tears began to fill her eyes as the excruciating pain assailed her. Did she have a choice? Apparently she did, for she fainted dead away once again.

"Doc!" Clayton cried. "Isn't there something ya can do for the pain? She's fainted again!"

"Settle down now, son. There's nothing outside of a good faint to help her while I clean this up. I'd be more concerned about how she's gonna take to her future husband up and shootin' his intended the moment he set eyes on her!"

Clayton sent a dagger of a glare to Spencer who stood watching over Doc Brown's shoulder as he cleaned the wound in the woman's foot. Just as he said, the bullet had only left a flesh wound, and thankfully Doc had been able to cut her boot off and remove the bullet as soon as he'd arrived.

"Will it heal properly?" Clayton asked, concerned, as he held the woman tightly to him again. She was in a sitting position on the desk, her upper body slightly turned and held against his belly and chest. Clayton held her at the one end while Doc sat at the desk and worked at the other.

"I did plenty of these during the war. This isn't the worst I've seen, but any type of wound can turn bad. I'll fix it up with a carbonic acid dressin' and that should do the trick. She'll be off it for a time. Hope you weren't plannin' on marryin' her right away 'cause I'm afraid your weddin' will have to be postponed. Unless, of course, she don't mind getting married while she's convalescin' in one of my patient rooms back at the house."

Clayton shook his head. "Don't worry about any of sort of marrying right now. Will she be okay?"

"I just done told ya she would. Now settle down, son. This should heal fine. In fact, you two oughta be able to get hitched come Christmas."

Clayton ran a hand over his weary face. Christmas? That meant the woman would be in Nowhere for weeks! So much for sending her back to wherever it was she came from … He again glared at his brother, who stood behind Doc Brown with an all-too-silly grin on his face. How many other folks in town knew of his so called *intended's* arrival that day?

Sheriff Clayton Riley was about to find out.

Summer opened her eyes slowly, awakened by the throbbing pain in her foot. She grimaced and squinted against the sunlight that streamed in through a nearby window.

"Ma'am?" a deep voice said, heavily laced with concern.

She turned her head toward the sound. Sitting in a chair in front of the window was the dark-haired man with the incredible green eyes. He was silhouetted against the autumn sun, but not so much so that she couldn't make out his features. He was tall even sitting, and his shoulders were broad, his arms strong as his biceps strained against the shirt he wore. He looked like some giant guardian angel without the wings, and if she wasn't in so much pain, she might consider a good swoon. In fact, she'd also welcome one if it meant she didn't have to put up with the pain in her foot any longer. So far swooning was the only thing that had worked …

"Ah, come around, have you?" an elderly looking man asked. He stood on the other side of the bed and held a glass of something in his hand. "Now be a good girl and drink this down. It'll help you sleep."

"Where am I?" she managed through gritted teeth.

"Nowhere," the green-eyed man said.

Something between a whimper and a chuckle escaped her and she looked to him. "That explains a lot. Who names a town Nowhere?"

"Well it's a long story. You see, back in '45 …" the elderly gentleman began.

"Doc, not now," the other man said.

She looked at the green-eyed man just as he turned to her. He was magnificent! Never had she seen anyone so handsome. In fact, she briefly wondered if he really *was* some sort of guardian angel and her intended was instead the elderly man who now tried to sit her up.

Once he got her there, he motioned for her to drink whatever was in the glass. She barely managed it, and with a cough and a sputter, turned once again to the guardian angel sitting on the other side of the bed. "I came here to get married," she told him.

His expression changed from concern to ... was that *guilt*? "I know."

"Where is Mr. Riley? I have to speak with Mr. Riley ..."

"Now you just rest and someone will be in later with your supper," the elderly man said.

"But ..."

Her guardian angel stood. "Quiet now. Do as Doc says and get your rest, ma'am. I'll see to ... Mr. Riley." His eyes narrowed slightly at the name and she came to the conclusion that she had yet to meet Sheriff Riley, her intended.

But where was he? Why hadn't he met the stage when it pulled up one door down from the sheriff's office? After debarking she took a moment to look for a man with a badge. As there was no sight of one, she'd taken up her satchel and headed toward his office. After all, a sheriff was a busy man and perhaps he'd been detained. Just as she was about to open the door, a man from the inside swung it wide and

BANG!

She remembered holding her eyes tightly shut against the pain as large hands grabbed her, lifted her up into strong arms and carried her inside, and then ...

"Oh ... you ... are you ...?"

The tall man's back was to her as he headed for the door. He looked bigger and broader now that he stood. He turned his head over his shoulder toward her, but didn't look at her. "Sleep now. We'll ... sort this out later when you're feeling better." He left, his spurs jangling across the wood floor and down the hall.

The elderly man tucked the blankets around her, put a hand to her forehead and looked down at her with a smile. "The wife'll be home soon – took a basket out to the Colson farm. Mrs. Colson ain't been feelin' too good lately, what with her expectin' a baby. As soon as she gets back she'll start supper. You rest until then, y'hear?"

"But Mr. Riley ..."

"Don't you worry your pretty little head about Mr. Riley. He'll be around." He winked at her, then quietly left the room, closing the door behind him.

Summer tried to relax, and let herself sink more deeply into the pillows. There was a floating sensation, and she closed her eyes to let it take her where it would. He must have given her some laudanum, and for that she was grateful. If she were to fall asleep her foot wouldn't pain her so.

But what did pain her was the elusive Sheriff

Riley. Where was he? Why hadn't he come for her? What was she to do if he wasn't here? But he had to be. The elderly gentleman said he was.

Summer's mind and heart gripped the thought and hung on. He had to be there, he just had to! He was her only hope.

"What are you gonna tell that little gal when she wakes up, Clayton? Don't tell me you're gonna load her up on a stage and send her packin'!"

Milly Brown's eyes were like fire. She glared at him like she used to when he was ten years old. She could be mighty scary when she wanted to be, and the middle-aged matron could give a look sure to scare the pants off of any misbehaving boy. Clayton wasn't a child anymore, but sure as he could spit, the woman *knew* he was misbehaving!

"Spencer answered the ad, not me," Clayton said in his defense. "What am I supposed to do? Let *him* marry her!"

"Keep your voice down, you sidewinder! She'll hear you!"

"I hope she does!"

"No, you don't! Think about what you're doin'! I've got a shot-up woman in there, no thanks to you, who thinks she's here to marry one Clayton Riley! What are *you* gonna tell her?"

Clayton tried to swallow, but his mouth had

gone dry. He couldn't get the girl's pain-filled face out of his mind. It was his fault she suffered so, his fault he was about to send her whole world crashing down, and his fault the entire town was now up in arms. More than one person gave him the eye when he'd left Doc Brown's place after getting the woman settled and headed back to the sheriff's office.

He absently rubbed his jaw a few times as he tried to figure a way out of the mess Spencer had gotten him into. Did the whole stinking town know? From the looks he got earlier, he was sure they did. But then how on God's green earth did *he* not know until the last minute?

Clayton was just going to have to face it. He would hang for the murder of his own brother …

"You gonna answer me, or you just gonna sit there wool gatherin'?" Milly pressed.

Clayton let go a long sigh as he belatedly remembered something. He reached into his vest pocket and pulled out his badge.

"Oh, you didn't!" Milly scolded. "Don't tell me you took that star off while you were in with that pretty little thing!"

Guilt's fist struck hard and fast as he pinned the badge on. "Milly, I …"

"Don't you 'Milly' me! You're gonna take this soup in there and face her like a man! In fact, *you're* gonna feed it to her!"

Clayton audibly gulped. He didn't know how the woman managed it, but he suddenly felt like his ten-year-old self again, like when he got caught stealing pears from Doc's prize tree and about to be given a good whipping. Only the woman down the hall wasn't a pear, and her life couldn't be so easily discarded as one. No, Milly was right – he had to talk with this Miss James and get things straightened out. The sooner, the better.

"Give me the tray," he said like a man about to have his last meal.

"Clayton Riley, look at you! What are you thinkin'? She's beautiful son, and she traveled all this way to marry you! If I were a man I wouldn't be thinkin' about packin' her up and sendin' her on her way! I'd be thankin' my brother for the blessin' he done give me!"

Clayton rubbed a hand over his tired face a few times before he again held out his hands. "Give me the tray, Milly. Let me get this over with."

"Fine," she huffed, and picked up the dinner tray she'd prepared. "But I think you'd be the biggest fool in the world if you sent her back! Just because you got your heart broken once don't mean it's gonna happen again!"

Clayton froze and fought the scathing retort he had at the ready. It was none of Milly's business! But ... he reminded himself, it was. Sarah had been Doc and Milly's daughter, after all. When she died, they all mourned – they'd lost a child while he'd lost a wife. It was the reason he'd quite apple farming and became the sheriff – Sarah had fallen out of one of the trees at harvest time and broken her neck.

And now he could have cared less if he ever saw another apple again. Unfortunately, the town was surrounded by them – acres and acres, in fact. The entire area was some of the best apple-producing country in the world, and his family had been in the business ever since they'd settled here, twenty years ago.

Clayton remembered how he'd dragged Spencer into upholding the law with him and made him his deputy, then leased out part of the land to Old Man Johnson to keep the farm going. Their mother hadn't been too happy about it, but they figured they could take better care of her that way. Besides, it was easier for their mother to manage – and with their pa having died a year before Sarah did, it gave her something to do. Leona Riley loved her farm, loved her apples and the land they owned. She wasn't about to give it up. Not like her eldest son had.

Now here he was: lonely, bitter, and the undisputed center of everyone's attention concerning the woman down the hall.

Clayton took the tray from Milly, turned on his boot heel, and headed for her room.

He balanced the tray on one hand and knocked on the door. It swung open a few inches and he peeked inside. The sun was setting and filled the room with a soft orange glow. It was beautiful to behold, and he almost dreaded it when he turned and looked at the woman lying on the bed.

He stifled a gasp as the sight that greeted him sent his toes to tingling. She *was* beautiful. Incredible!

Why had he not seen her like this before?

Probably because he was too busy feeling guilty for accidently shooting her. But the sight of her slumbering form chased the unwanted emotion away only to replace it with one even more dangerous: compassion.

He couldn't help himself. Like an injured little lamb, she lay in perfect stillness upon the bed, the golden glow of the setting sun making her complexion look downright peachy. Her dark lashes were long and in stark contrast to the creamy smoothness of her skin. Her blonde hair had come loose from its pins, and long tendrils had fanned out on either side of her head upon the pillows.

Clayton closed his eyes against the unwanted emotions that welled up from deep within. He tried to steel himself against them, and failed miserably. Loneliness wrapped its ugly fingers around his heart and began to squeeze …

He drew in a deep breath and set the tray down upon a nearby table. The practical side of him said he should wake her and see to it she got something to eat before the soup got cold. The other side (what side *that* was, he had no idea) said he should stand there and drink her in, every last beautiful inch. From the top of her head to the toes of her …

Practicality was quick to interrupt and remind him he'd shot her, not far from those toes.

Clayton sighed, reached over, and gave the pretty little thing's shoulder a gentle shake.

THREE

Summer's eyes opened slowly. She heard someone moan, and hazily realized it was her.

Another sound caught her attention, and she turned her head to find a man – a *very large* man – standing over the bed, bathed in a beautiful golden light. Her angel ... She smiled at him.

Had she died, then? No, no – she couldn't have. For one, she smelled chicken soup; for another, there was the dull throbbing pain in her foot. This man had to be the one she woke up to earlier, the man who had come to her rescue at the sheriff's office, and therefore not an angel. "Hello," she said softly, and decided she'd think of him as her guardian angel anyway.

He took a nearby chair and carefully sat, then looked at her and swallowed hard, as if he couldn't believe what he was seeing. Was something else wrong with her and they hadn't told her about it? She looked worriedly up at the ceiling before letting her gaze once again drift in his direction.

"Are you all right?" he asked, concerned.

"Are you in much pain?"

She looked up at him. "It hurts, but not like before." She tried to swallow, but her throat was incredibly dry. She licked her lips, which didn't help much either.

He quickly glanced around. "Let me help you," he said as he got up from the chair and went to a water pitcher and glass sitting atop a dresser. He poured her a drink and came back to the bed, gently helped her to sit up, and held the glass to her lips.

She took a few small sips, then drank greedily. She hadn't realized how thirsty she was. But her desire wasn't only for water.

What Summer James really wanted most was freedom: freedom from her life at the orphanage, freedom from back-breaking work to help Mrs. Teeters keep the impoverished establishment open, freedom from the Mr. Slades of the world. She had loved the woman and her fellow orphans, but her time there had come to an end by law. It was as if the stars had aligned against her to drive her out of her home and her hometown, and during the long train ride to Salt Lake she'd wondered if the law hadn't conspired with the likes of Mr. Slade to ensure such men would have plenty of women to fill the beds of their patrons. The thought turned her stomach and she grimaced.

"Are you okay? I can get the doctor if you want," the big man said in a rush.

"I'll live," she said and turned to look at him. His eyes were darker, almost stormy in their depths, as they caught hers in a heated gaze. She stopped breathing at the look of concern on his face and gasped.

With his eyes still glued to hers, he scooted off the bed and into the chair. "I … have your dinner," he said suddenly. "You'd best eat something."

She slowly nodded. She was hungry, and remembered she'd not eaten anything since the night before. She'd been so nervous she couldn't think about food when it came time for breakfast that morning at the stage's stop-over station. She tried to sit up, only to moan in pain, the movement causing her foot to throb terribly.

"Whoa there! Let me get a hold of ya now," he said and lifted her so she sat up straight. She looked at him as the heat of his hands burned through her blouse to the skin beneath. His hands were large, his fingers spread against her ribcage.

They stared at one another a moment before he slowly pulled away and released her. Did he feel it too – the bolt of sensation that traveled through her entire body to settle in the pit of her stomach and chase any thoughts of Slade and his evil lot away? She certainly hoped so …

He turned to the tray and picked up a bowl of soup. He started to hand it to her, then stopped. She could tell his mind was at work, could see it in his eyes. Slowly he reached for the spoon on the tray, picked it up, set it in the bowl, then smiled as his eyes took on a look she'd never seen before. It sent her insides to melting as he scooped up a spoonful of soup and very carefully offered it to her.

She swallowed hard as her breathing stopped. Good heavens – he was going to feed her?! Surely she could manage a bowl of soup on her own! Or could she? The slightest movement shot pain through her foot.

"Take a bite." His voice was soft and low. "I know you'll like it – Milly's a great cook."

Her mouth began to water, but was it from the soup he offered or the look on his face? He seemed so confident, so in control. Well, in this case he *did* hold the spoon, so she supposed that was understandable …

"C'mon, try it," he coaxed, his voice dropping another notch. Its deep rolling sound sent a delicious tingle up her spine.

She gingerly leaned forward a few inches and opened her mouth. Ever so carefully, he fed her the first taste of the most wonderful chicken soup she'd ever had.

She licked her lips, breathed deeply, and eagerly opened her mouth again.

He stiffened slightly, and she noticed how the muscles in his arms tightened. But he scooped up another spoonful and repeated the process. It was the best bowl of soup Summer could remember - in more ways than one!

Good Lord! Whoever thought chicken soup could undo a man so effortlessly – especially when he wasn't even the one eating it! Every time he gave her a spoonful, his body tightened with every unsatisfied fiber of his being. But it wasn't lust – this went deeper than that. This was a soul-searing need to be with a woman, *this* woman, to meld into one with her, to be a part of something bigger and better than himself.

He'd forgotten what it felt like to *want* to love someone, to desire a life together, to battle all of life's storms as partners. In a flash, he saw himself married to the woman sitting on the bed before him, so helpless and vulnerable. The thought that she'd traveled all this way to do just that was like a fist in his gut. He didn't deserve her. He'd been all too ready to load her up like some parcel and send her back to wherever his conniving brother had found her ...

Speaking of Spencer, where was he? Clayton hadn't seen him since carrying the woman to Doc's house that afternoon.

He turned to her, and realized his mouth was hanging open like some lovesick dote. He snapped it shut and tried to scoop up another spoonful of soup but it was all gone. She looked longingly at the spoon, then at him. Her blue eyes were wide and he fought against a smile. Did she think he was handsome? Of course, the Riley brothers were probably the best-looking things in this part of the territory, and they both well knew it. But this was the first woman since Sarah, whom he *wanted* to have think he was handsome. In fact, he suddenly realized he felt a little nervous at the thought she might not.

He fidgeted in the chair and set down the

bowl, then looked back to her.

"I … I suppose you're to thank for taking care of me?" she asked.

Her voice came out a beautiful soft lilt. He began to have visions of the stage pulling out, her weeping from having been forced upon it by his own hand. He unconsciously balled one hand into a fist. Good Lord, what was he going to do? Punch *himself* for being an idiot? "I, um, reckon so," he said as his heart beat a little faster.

She was small, smaller than Sarah and more delicately built. He fought the urge to move a stray lock of hair away from her face.

"I have to thank you, then. I don't know what I would have done had you not acted so quickly and fetched the doctor."

He smiled. Her gratitude was genuine, her eyes full of it. Against his better judgment, he reached out and brushed the stray lock aside.

It was his undoing. The moment his finger touched her skin, her eyes closed and her head tilted slightly back. Heat filled him, and he thought he might shoot straight up into the air and right through the roof. His finger felt as if it had been seared by the sheer softness of her skin.

Her breathing slowed and she opened her eyes. "Who are you?" she asked on a breathy whisper.

He closed his own eyes as the battle for his heart raged for several excruciating seconds. In theory he could say nothing, get up, leave the room, and have Spencer take care of the whole business – make *him* play nursemaid to the girl, see to it *he* took care of all the travel arrangements for her return to …

… oh, for Pete's sake! He didn't even know where she came from!

"Sir? Please … who are you?"

Clayton opened his eyes. The look on her face was one of pure innocence and trust. It was all he could do not to groan as one side of his soul won out.

He sighed, smiled, and slowly said, "Well … I'm Sheriff Clayton Riley, ma'am. And I'm … I'm to be your husband."

"*You're* Clayton Riley?" Her eyes flew to his chest, and there it was – a silver star. How did she not notice it earlier? Where had it been? Surely she would have seen it. But she *had* been in great pain, and then the doctor had given her the laudanum … she stared at him in disbelief. *This* was Clayton Riley? Her very own guardian angel – *he'd* sent for her?

But … but what if now that he saw her, he didn't want her? She understood it could happen – Solomon had explained it to her the day he came to fetch her from Winslow and escort her to the train. Some men sent a bride back, for whatever reason. If that were to happen, she was to immediately let Mrs. Ridgley know, so Solomon or Jethro could meet her at the train station. But Mrs. Ridgley was confident

Summer would not be coming back to New Orleans.

At least there'd been no sign of that nasty Mr. Slade as Solomon escorted her to the station and sent her on her way. She'd rested easier once she was on the train, but Solomon warned her nonetheless to keep a sharp eye out. At least as far as Colorado – then she should be safe.

Solomon's instructions frightened her. Would a man go that far to procure another slave for his establishment? But Jethro and Solomon knew well what a man like Slade would do; they had been *his* slaves before the war broke out. They'd gained their freedom with the help of Mrs. Ridgley, when she too had broken away and cut all ties with the likes of Slade.

But enough of that. She came here to get married, and by heaven she was going to see it through, no matter what Mr. Riley thought of her. But surely, with the way he was looking at her, he must be pleased with what he saw – at least a little ...

She swallowed hard and caught his gaze. "So Mr. Riley," she began, "when do we get married?"

Clayton's eyes widened as he froze. Did he hear her right? Did she just ask when they were getting married? *Oh, good God, maybe you should lock yourself up for being an imbecile!*

Of course that's what she's asking! It's what she came out here for, isn't it? He offered her a sheepish grin. Yes, of course it was. And now that he'd told her who he was, there was no backing out. *Do these mail-order bride contracts have a release clause?* He wondered.

"Mr. Riley? Is something wrong?"

He jumped at the sound of her voice. "Yes," he choked out. "I mean, no! No, it's just that ... considering your injury, I think we should postpone it ... for a time ..."

Her eyes misted and her lower lip trembled ever so slightly.

Oh, no! Don't cry, PLEASE don't cry! I can't take tears! He smiled through clenched teeth as he stared down at her. "I just thought you might want to be able to stand when we ..." *say it, c'mon, say it!* "... get married."

She sighed in relief.

Was she worried that he didn't want to marry her? Clayton rolled his eyes and slapped himself on the forehead. *Idiot! Of course that's what she thinks! And with some reason ...*

"Mr. Riley?"

"Oh! I, ah, forgot to tell Ma you're here. I'd best get out to the house and let her know. She'll be very excited to meet you, I'm sure."

"Are you?"

Clayton swallowed, looked her in the eye, and took a deep breath. Her eyes misted again and her face paled. *Riley, you cad! Man up! Listen to those around you! Who has a better head right now, you or someone like Milly? You've been lonely for months! Look at her.*

Look *at her!*

He swallowed again. "Lord, but you're beautiful."

She blushed a bright pink.

The sight made him smile. "I'm sorry, but I haven't been myself lately …" Shame hit hard and fast as he stood and turned toward the window. Heaven forbid if she saw how rotten he was. Didn't he just make up his mind this marriage would be good for him? Yet here he was, already trying to figure a way out of it.

What are you afraid of Riley? Really, what is it?

"I'm sorry you haven't been yourself. I know this arrangement isn't the usual way it's done," she said then added, "Why, we didn't even get the chance to exchange any letters."

He suddenly turned to her. "We didn't?"

She shook her head. "No – at least I hadn't been given any. The only thing I have is a copy of the marriage contract I signed."

He tried to remain calm. What had Spencer gotten him into? He figured his mischievous brother had been writing to the girl for a few months at least. "May I see it?"

"Certainly – it's in my satchel. If you could bring it here …"

Clayton looked around the room and spied the satchel sitting on the floor near the dresser. He picked it up and brought it to her.

She took it from him, opened it and dug through the contents. Clayton noticed it was nearly empty. Did she have a trunk somewhere that needed to be brought out to the farm?

"Where are your other belongings?"

She stopped her digging and looked up at him. "This … this is all I have."

His eyes widened slightly as he looked in the satchel. He could see a dress, a comb, and a small Bible, but that was all.

She pulled out the marriage contract and handed it to him. Clayton noticed she didn't look at him when she did so. She was embarrassed by her lack of possessions. *She doesn't even have a wedding dress, poor little thing.*

He took the contract from her and began to read. So, Miss Summer James was from New Orleans … but no letters? Nothing? She just signed a contract, hopped on a train and now here she was? How could that be?

"Miss James, did I send a picture?"

She raised her brow at that. "You don't remember?"

He shrugged. "It was … a while ago." At least he guessed it had been a while since Spencer sent a picture, if he sent one at all.

"Yes, you did." She reached into her satchel again and pulled out the Bible, opened it up and took out a small photograph from between the pages.

Clayton shook himself. *Spencer is going to die!* It was the photo his mother kept in a double frame atop her dresser in her room. Did she know it was missing? Good grief, maybe she was the one that gave it to Spencer! "May I see that?"

She handed it to him. He took it and examined it. Yep, it was the one from his mother's room, all right. His own blood stained the back. He'd cut himself taking it out of an old frame to put it into the new one. "It's a little old," he began. "Sorry it's not a very good representation."

"That's all right. You didn't even get a picture of me. I … I realize how great a disappointment I could have been … if … if you didn't …"

"Think you were pretty?"

She swallowed as her cheeks turned pink. But was she simply being humble, or was she truly ashamed of how she looked? Clayton's heart dropped into his stomach at the thought. She was the most beautiful woman he had ever seen! Oh, what was he thinking? Who wouldn't be pleased with someone so lovely, who'd traveled all this way without a lick of correspondence between them? Not only that, but who would be willing to marry a man with nothing but an old photograph and the word of the mail-order bride service as to his character? He sure the Sam blazes wouldn't if *he* had been a bride!

Suddenly his lawman's instincts kicked in and he found himself once again sitting in the chair next to the bed, his body leaning toward her as his mind ran wild with questions. Clayton had to follow his gut on something.

"Miss James, might I be the first to say I think you are one of the most beautiful women I have ever seen, so please don't think I'm

disappointed in that regard. But I do have to ask
… are you running from something?"

FOUR

Summer froze. No! She couldn't tell him! What would he do if he found out she'd spent most of her life in an orphanage? That she'd barely gotten out of New Orleans? That had she stayed, she'd be good for nothing more than …

She turned her face away as tears stung the back of her eyes. How could she tell him? Of course she was running – running from a life of slavery and servitude to men who would use her up in a matter of years and cast her aside like a piece of garbage. And she wasn't the only one. What of the others, the girls soon to come of age who also faced the horrors of leaving the safe confines of the orphanage? Would Mrs. Ridgley be able to get them away in time as well?

Large fingers gently touched her chin and pulled her head around to face him. His own face was an expressionless mask, unreadable. But when her first tear finally fell, it was met with a compassion she had never seen in any man's eyes.

He let go of her chin and gently brushed the tear away. "I guess this answers my question," he whispered as he stood. He put the marriage contract into the satchel, placed the bag back on the floor by the dresser, and slowly turned to her. "I'll make what arrangements I have to, and as soon as Doc says you're ready, I'll come for you."

Summer could only stare as her entire body went numb. He was going to send her back. *Oh, good God, no!*

He looked about, then chuckled to himself. "Guess I done left my hat and coat in the kitchen. I'll let Milly know what's going on. You rest now." He smiled and left the room.

Summer shook her head. *Oh, no! No, no, no, no!* She couldn't go back – Slade would be on her quicker than flies on sugar! And when he got ahold of her he'd *never* let go! He'd make sure that once he had her entrenched into the life he planned for her there would be no escape.

She stifled a sob as she heard muffled voices from down the hall and then listened to the front door as it opened and closed. She quickly looked to the window, the golden light of sunset nearly gone now, and watched as Clayton Riley strolled down the front walk, through the gate, and out of sight.

"Oh, please, Lord! I can't leave! I can't go back!" What would she do? Where could she go? One thing was for certain: until her foot healed, she wasn't going anywhere.

Perhaps that was it! Maybe so long as her foot was injured he couldn't send her back!

Summer's shoulders slumped. Who was she kidding? She couldn't fake her injury to stay.

No, that wouldn't do at all. *Think, Summer, think!*

She closed her eyes and took a few deep breaths ... then suddenly smiled. Of course! She'd make plans of her own - either to stay on in Nowhere or go someplace close by where she could find a job and earn the money it had cost Mr. Riley to bring her out west in the first place. It was, after all, the logical thing to do.

She took one more breath to calm down before she smiled with relief. Surely Mr. Riley would understand her dilemma and cooperate, wouldn't he? Or wait – was Mrs. Ridgley to reimburse him based upon her return to New Orleans? Good Lord, what if *that* was how it worked? She had seen something in the marriage contract like that ... but her head was so fuzzy at the moment she couldn't remember the exact wording.

Her eyes suddenly fixed on the satchel next to the dresser. How was she going to get over there to check? She looked to her foot beneath the light blanket that covered her. To move meant pain, and she didn't want to risk further injury. She turned her head toward the door. Wasn't there someone else in the house with her? Milly, was it? Perhaps she could get it for her?

Summer let her body fall back against the pillows, suddenly too tired to think about it further. She'd call the woman in and have her fetch it for her, yes, but first she wanted to close her eyes against the pain in her foot for a moment. After she rested she'd tackle the task at hand …

But before she could so much as think about what she would do if the contract did indeed state she had to go back, sleep took her from all her troubles and pain once more.

Five days passed with no sign of Clayton Riley. Or his brother, for that matter – Summer remembered the man who briefly introduced himself before rushing out of the sheriff's office to get help the day she got shot. But they were absent for a good reason. Milly, the doctor's wife, told her they'd had to hurry out of town to join a posse – they were tracking a gang of outlaws that had struck a settlement south of Nowhere.

Summer's stomach had been in knots ever since. Would they catch them? Would the Riley brothers get hurt? What if Mr. Riley didn't come back at all? Then what would she do? She silently chastised herself for thinking such morbid thoughts.

Instead of worrying about the Rileys, she concentrated on how she could carry out her own plans. Firstly, the marriage contract *did* state that should the groom not find his bride to his liking, he could send her back to New Orleans and all funds would be reimbursed to him. The Ridgley Mail-Order Bride Service would send him another candidate, but it would cost him an additional fee on top of the train and stage fare. Perhaps that was a fail-safe – if a man knew he had to pay an extra fee to get another bride, he'd be more apt to keep the one he originally got. But that wasn't going to do her much good – she needed to avoid going back at all costs.

Secondly, she'd discovered the local mercantile was in need of help. As soon as she was able to walk, she'd go talk with Mr. Quinn, the owner, about a job. Surely, with what skills she had, she could be hired. Her only worry was her foot, which kept her from inquiring in the first place. By the time it was healed enough for her to do so, the position might already be filled.

Thus thirdly, she had found there were several other small settlements within a fifty-mile radius of Nowhere. She could probably make it to one of them … but then what?

Which brought Summer right back to square one. Again. And again. And again.

She threw her face in her hands and moaned. Right when she thought she'd found a solution, something came to mind that told her it wouldn't work. One more go-around and she thought she might scream.

If only she didn't feel so utterly trapped! The only good thing to happen in the last few days was that her foot didn't hurt as much. That, at least, was encouraging. On the other hand, as soon as it was healed, Clayton Riley would likely toss her onto a stage the first chance he got. Her mind strayed to a picture of him storming into the room, scooping her up into his arms, and carrying her straight to a waiting coach. He'd give her a "good bye and good luck" before he waved at the driver. And she'd be off, back to a nightmare she'd been trying to avoid ever since she was old enough to realize the world was full of scoundrels.

"And so few good men," she whispered to herself. Her eyes wandered around the room. "Clayton Riley, why? Why don't you want me?"

But what could she expect? There had been no correspondence, no letters of warmth and happy words to let him get to know her. He not only had got her sight unseen, but unread as well.

If only she could find a job, earn enough to send to Mrs. Ridgley to cover the reimbursement money, and make things work that way. But Clayton Riley was a man of the law. He would do things by the book, she was sure.

Summer sank against the pillows as if to hide. There was no way out, no way around any of it. Her only hope was to seek refuge with Mrs. Ridgley for as long as she could.

What a shame, what a crying shame he didn't want her! The one decent man she'd met in years! And he had to go and be a lawman that didn't want a woman with any sort of past. Well, everyone has a past. He just didn't want one that wasn't to his standards. He didn't even bother to ask what she was running from! Once he figured it out he immediately came to the conclusion she simply wouldn't do.

Men – they could be such beasts! Such

horrible, *horrible* beasts! What was a woman to do? Her fate was in Clayton Riley's hands, and once back in New Orleans it would only be a matter of time before she would be grabbed by the hands of one man or another – if not the vile Mr. Slade, then some other flesh-peddler.

The war on slavery, it seemed, still raged on. Only this slave trade had been going on long before the war so recently fought by the North and the South. If only she'd been born a man, then she'd show Clayton Riley what for!

Speaking of Clayton Riley, was that him coming up the walk?

"Oh God, no!" Summer said under her breath as she looked frantically about the room. But what could she do? Where could she go? She couldn't even stand on her own two feet! She was indeed completely and utterly at the man's mercy. He had probably come to tell her he'd telegraphed Mrs. Ridgley to say he was sending her back. She slumped against her pillows as her heart sank in defeat.

A knock sounded at the front door, but she ignored it. All her life she'd been rejected, tossed aside or left behind. Why should this be any different? No wonder Mr. Slade and his kind preyed upon hers. Who else wanted her?

She could hear Milly greet him, hear his spurs jangle as he came into the house …

No. No! NO! No matter what happened, she wasn't going to let anyone – not Clayton Riley, not Mr. Slade – tell her she was worthless! So what if Mr. High-and-Mighty Sheriff Clayton Riley didn't want her? God wanted her! By golly, yes, He did – and she would keep that hidden in her heart to see her through the long journey back.

"Miss James?"

Summer steeled herself one more time before she looked at him as he entered the room.

"Oh!" she suddenly cried as he pulled the blanket off her, and then scooped her into his arms without warning. "What are you *doing*?!"

"I'm sorry about this, Miss James, but I've got a schedule to keep, and Doc needs the bed. Milly!"

Milly came into the room and quickly snatched up Summer's satchel. Summer wasn't the only patient occupying the doctor's three patient rooms. Several men had been wounded hunting the outlaws and brought in not a day after the posse left! Milly had been busy with them ever since, and had hardly had time to say two words to her in the days that followed.

Summer knew what was happening. Why else would Milly be holding her satchel and tagging along behind Mr. Riley as he carried her down the hall? Oh, no! No, it couldn't be! "Mr. Riley, please!"

"I'm sorry about this, Miss James, but I don't see any help for it."

"But Mr. Riley …" No! She would *not* cry! After all, she had known this was going to happen.

"Oh, it's not as bad as all that!" Milly admonished as she followed them out the front door. "Lots of mail-order brides have to do this. You'll be fine once you get there."

"Once I get there?!" Summer squealed. "But my foot's not even healed yet!"

"What has that got to do with anything?" Milly scolded. "Stop your fussing, child, and be grateful Sheriff Riley was able to make arrangements so quickly!"

"But …"

"I'll not hear another word about it, Miss James," Mr. Riley told her in a stern voice. His arms were incredibly strong, and he carried her down the street without effort. "It's all been arranged."

Summer couldn't help it as her exhaustion and frustration caught up with her. She began to cry. He was sending her off without a second thought, and she couldn't even walk! How cruel could the man be?

Too tired and downhearted to argue further, she turned her head into his shoulder and sobbed out her shame and heartache. Besides, people were watching them, and she couldn't stand the humiliation of the ordeal. Now the whole town would know he didn't want her!

She finally glanced up and saw the stage and its driver waiting for them. She never thought she'd *ever* be one to beg, but now she was considering it.

The driver of the stagecoach smiled and waved at them as they drew closer. Mr. Riley gave him a curt nod of acknowledgement.

Summer could stand it no longer. "Please, Mr. Riley, please, I can't! I just can't! Please don't make me go!"

He stopped. "What are you so upset about? A

man's gotta do what a man's gotta do! Doc, Milly and I all discussed it, and we felt this was the best thing all the way around."

Maybe it was the laudanum. Maybe it was simply the fatigue at spending each waking moment trying to figure out a way to keep what was happening now from happening at all. Whatever it was, it caused every pent-up emotion she'd stuffed down inside herself over the last few days to suddenly erupt. She wished with all her might she could stop – it was humiliating. But she couldn't.

"For the love of God, woman!" Mr. Riley exclaimed. "You'd think I was taking you to hang!"

Summer tried to speak but couldn't, the sobbing was that bad.

"Whacha do, Sheriff?" the stagecoach driver asked. "Accidently shoot her again?"

"No! Now move aside so I can get her settled."

Summer sucked big gulps of air, so much so she felt as if she might be sick. She did her best to wipe away her tears as the awful, beastly, *horrible* Mr. Riley made his way straight to the …

"What?" Summer exclaimed, her despair suddenly flashing into anger. "*You* were the one who shot me? You beast! You cur!" she screamed, and began to flail away at him with her fists. She was so enraged, she didn't even notice that he'd walked past the stagecoach to a wagon parked just beyond it.

"Stop it, woman! What are you, crazy?"

Clayton had to stop walking just to keep from dropping her as she tried to cuff him around. "I told you I made arrangements! What are you so upset about? It's not like its improper or anything!"

"Improper?" Summer screeched. "Who are you to talk about what's improper?" She tried to take another swing at his head.

Clayton caught her wrist before her hand could connect. "Stop it! Look, it was an accident, all right? I dropped my gun! Now how are we supposed to take care of you if you're screaming and fighting like a woman possessed?"

The words "take care of you" somehow penetrated the fog of rage around her brain. "Wh-what?" She blinked, and suddenly realized he wasn't putting her on the stagecoach as she'd assumed. "What … what exactly are you … doing?"

Clayton was finally able to reach the back of the wagon. Spencer was there, watching them warily as he tossed some blankets into the wagon bed, then jumped up himself.

"Isn't it obvious, you silly woman? I'm taking you home!"

"Home?" Not New Orleans?

"Yes, home! *My* home! Now do you think you can stop knocking me around for a minute?"

FIVE

Summer thought she might faint. Not the stage. Home. *His* home. And soon … her home too?

She stared numbly at Clayton Riley as Spencer quickly spread the blankets over some hay. Mr. Riley stared right back, his jaw set as he shook his head, then gently handed her up to his brother's outstretched arms. Without saying a word, Spencer settled her onto the waiting blankets, covered her with several more, then climbed over the wagon seat and sat.

Mr. Riley took the satchel from Milly, tossed it into the wagon, then hopped up himself and sat beside her. He looked down at her briefly before he tucked the blankets in more tightly, then put an arm around her and pulled her against him. "Let's go," he said, his jaw set as before.

Summer audibly gulped. "I … I thought …"

"You thought what? I'd really like to know, because I've never seen someone make such a fuss over having to give up their room to a couple of wounded men. But they're my men and I want them cared for proper."

"Your men were hurt?" she asked on a whisper, still not over the shock of not being sent away.

"Shot, unfortunately. Feel bad about it, but at least they're not dead. Both are married."

She stared at him, her mouth open in a continued state of utter disbelief. "You're taking me to … your house, then?"

Mr. Riley looked at her, his face now a mask of concern mixed with something else. Was he about to laugh at her? He held her to him a bit tighter and yelled. "Don't bother sparing the horses, Spencer – let's get on home!"

Good grief! What had Doc given her? She was acting plumb loco! Crying, sobbing, carrying on like he was … oh no, it couldn't be …

He chanced a look at her and loosened his grip. He was trying to keep her warm, but he'd also feared she might try to jump out of the wagon, what with the crazy way she was going on. Either way, he'd figured he'd best keep a tight hold on her. But what woman wouldn't try to make a break for it if she thought he was going to load her up onto the stage, injured as she was, and send her away?

Oh, Lord, how could she think such a thing? Didn't I tell her I'd make all the arrangements?

But had he really? And even if he had, had he

told her what "the arrangements" were?

He'd spent the last five days getting shot at and trying to keep himself and his men in one piece. Making plans to transport Miss James to the farm hadn't exactly been at the forefront of his mind. When he got back that morning he'd hurried home, gotten cleaned up, spoke with his mother and brother, then went into town to gather up what he needed – namely, the woman sitting next to him, who looked like she didn't know whether she was going to laugh or cry hysterically.

Either one, he decided, would be bad. If she laughed hysterically, she might well *be* loco. If she cried, he'd have to climb up front with Spencer. If there was one thing Clayton Riley couldn't stand, it was a crying woman. Carrying her to the wagon might have done him in, and having her try to knock him senseless hadn't helped either. To realize she was sobbing – and fighting – like that was because she thought he was sending her away was harder to choke down now than when it was actually happening.

How on earth had he not explained it? But then, he'd been in such a hurry to find Spencer, to send word to the mail-order bride company that Miss James had arrived, to do a little detective work … he might not have explained a thing. He couldn't remember. What he did remember was that she came to Nowhere because she was running from something. He was no Pinkerton, but he had a nose for finding things out.

He glanced at her again. Once he got her

settled at the farm, he'd find out a thing or two about his future bride.

Clayton pushed back his hat and allowed himself a moment to relax. Miss James was calm for the time being, but she did look a fright, though. Her eyes were puffy and red, her nose much the same. He wondered if they should stop at the creek and clean her up before their mother saw her. But Ma would probably make a bigger fuss if she found out they had. It was getting downright cold out, and would probably snow later.

No, he'd have to carry Miss James into the house and face the music like a man. And then, of course, pray his mother and brother could keep their mouths shut that he'd had no idea Miss James had been sent to be his future bride in the first place. Seemed the whole town knew, but by a sheer miracle no one had said a word to the poor woman. Probably because it was a lot more fun to watch him squirm. Milly and Doc had kept everyone away for the most part – but then, Milly and Doc were also the worst! Especially Milly, who threatened him the day he left with the posse from Northridge that she might accidently spill the beans. For a front seat at his wedding, though, she'd keep her mouth shut.

Clayton shook his head and smiled at the thought as Spencer drove on.

They reached the house without further incident, and Spencer pulled up to the front porch. Their mother came running out, her face lit with pure delight, and went straight for them.

"At last! Land sakes, I thought you'd never get here!"

Spencer set the brake and hopped down. "Actually, we made excellent time. Clayton couldn't wait to get home, could you, Clayton?"

Clayton unwrapped his arm from around the trembling woman at his side and glared at his brother, then looked to her. "You okay? You're shaking like a leaf."

Her teeth began to chatter. "I … I'm … it's just…"

He bent his head to hers, his voice low. "I'm sorry for the misunderstanding, Miss James. How could you think I would …?"

"Stop dawdling, Clayton! Let me see my new daughter-in-law!" his mother cried from the porch.

Clayton sighed. "She's not your daughter-in-law yet, Ma. She's gotta heal up first."

"All the more reason to get her off that dusty old pile of hay and bring her inside. It's freezing out here! Hurry up now!"

"I'm sorry to be so much trouble, Mr. Riley," Miss James said in a soft voice.

"Stop. I'll hear none of it. You thought I was sending you back, and did … well, I suppose if I was a woman in that situation, I might wail like a coyote too."

Her eyes flashed at his words, and for some reason he was glad he'd gotten a burr under her saddle. It sure beat seeing her all teary-eyed and sniffling. Sarah had been at her best when she'd gotten feisty …

Before she could comment, Spencer had

climbed over the seat and into the wagon bed. Clayton moved away from Miss James and hopped out to give his brother room. Spencer carefully picked her up, blankets and all, and handed her down to him.

"I am sorry for the misunderstanding. It was my fault – I should have made myself clearer," he told her again as he headed for the porch where his mother waited.

She said nothing, only stared at him with those big blue eyes, her body spent from her earlier panic. She was limp in his arms, her head against his shoulder as he went up the porch steps, clearly exhausted. And it was entirely his fault.

"My word, what's happened to the poor girl? You boys didn't drive that team too fast, did you? Why, she looks like someone beat her with a stick." *Ouch!* Ma always did have a way with words, but did she have to put it like that? "Bring her inside, Clayton! Hurry up now!"

He followed his mother into the warm house, down the hall and into a small office they'd converted to a bedroom earlier that afternoon. Mrs. Charles Riley wasn't about to risk further injury to her future daughter-in-law by having her stumble down the stairs with an injured foot!

"Set her on the bed, Clayton. That's it, careful now …"

"She's not going to break, Ma," Clayton told her in a tired voice.

"She already *is* broken – be careful!"

Now that he thought on it, he was as tired as Miss James looked – maybe more so. The last three days had been long and hard. Topping it off with a frightened woman who thought him to be the lowest varmint in the territory hadn't improved matters. But he'd make it up to her, though he didn't know how just yet. Maybe Spencer could help ... in fact, Spencer *better* help, as he was the one who'd gotten him into this mess in the first place! Worse still, it was their mother's idea to send away for a mail-order bride – she'd better pitch in some too!

"There now ... that's better, isn't it, dear? You just stay right there while I go fix you a little snack before supper. I'm sure Doc and Milly didn't fill you up with anything but soup while you were at their place!" His mother turned and happily left the room. One would think Clayton had just given her a new toy! Perhaps after a day or two, she'd calm down, but the more he thought on it, he didn't think so. Sarah had left a void in his mother's life too. She was the daughter his mother had never had, and Ma had suffered the loss when she died just as hard as everyone else.

But this wasn't Sarah on the bed staring up at him with her jaw set now in pure determination. In fact, the woman's look was so grim, he began to worry what sort of thoughts she was harboring in that pretty head of hers ... and whether they involved cuffing him around again.

"I'll ... go get your bag," he told her and turned toward the door.

"Mr. Riley." It was a declaration, not an inquiry.

"Yes?" he asked without turning around.

"Thank you."

Now he did face her. "For what?"

"For not sending me away. I promise I'll make you a good wife."

Her words were spoken evenly, void of emotion. Where was the wailing, sobbing, frightened little thing that had threatened to tear his heart out?

He once again turned to the doorway. "I'm sure you will." And with that, he left the room.

"Here you are, some nice molasses cookies – made them this morning, I did! I hope you like them!" Mrs. Riley set a plate of cookies and a glass of milk down on a desk next to the small bed. "I hope you'll be comfortable in here until you can sleep up in Clayton's room. This used to be my husband's office. The boys use it now, of course, but I thought it would serve you best for the time being."

Summer couldn't help the blush that crept into her cheeks at the mention of Clayton's room. But then, where else would she be sleeping once they were married?

She set the thought aside and looked at the woman standing before her. Mrs. Riley had a generous build but wasn't fat. She had bright blue eyes that sparkled, and what must have once been a glorious head of blonde hair. Now heavily streaked with grey, she wore it loosely piled on top of her head, and Summer wondered how long it was. She had a pleasant lilt to her voice, and there was a wonderful smell about her, as if she'd been baking cookies outside the house rather than inside.

Summer had been given her name because she was born on the first day of said season and left on Winslow's doorstep. But she thought Mrs. Riley could have been named for spring. Everything about her seemed fresh and new, and Summer could tell by the animated way the woman talked that she was full of life.

Summer's eyes darted about the room. Who wouldn't be full of life and love in a house like this? Everything was neat and orderly – *pristine*, that was the word! – yet so homey and warm at the same time.

She looked back to Mrs. Riley. "Thank you for allowing me to stay here."

Mrs. Riley looked at her in shock. "My dear sweet child, you're going to *live* here! You don't have to thank me for it! If anyone, thank Spence ...oh, silly me, I'm forever getting those two boys mixed up – thank *Clayton* for bringing you out here."

Summer blinked a few times. How could she get her sons mixed up with something like marriage? Didn't she know which one of them had sent away for a mail-order bride?

"Oh, but you must be tired! I'll leave you to rest, then have Clayton bring you to the table when supper's ready."

Summer smiled and nodded, her eyes heavy. The incident in town had drained her strength, and it was hitting her harder now that she knew she would be alone for a time. "Thank you, Mrs. Riley. I think I will rest awhile."

"You do that, dear. I'll send Clayton just as soon as it's time to eat." She backed out of the room and closed the door.

Summer let go a long, weary sigh. What must her future husband think of her now, what with the way she'd carried on? What indeed? As she recalled, he'd compared her to a wailing coyote! But she supposed they could have gotten off to a much rougher start ... *rougher start, my foot! Literally – the man shot you as soon as you got off the stage!* Yes, there was that ...

But the alternative to having her future husband accidently shoot her, fail to tell her of his plans not to send her away, and of course let her make a fool of herself in front of everyone (okay, so maybe she did that on her own) was to live as a slave in a world where men dominated and women were bought and sold like cattle. New Orleans had been a den of slavery for decades, and would probably continue to be unless someone put a stop to it. In the meantime, people like Mrs. Ridgley and Mrs. Teeters did whatever they could to ensure at least some women got out before they were snatched up and put into the waiting chains of guilt and shame.

She closed her eyes and waited for the throbbing in her foot to subside before trying to move into a more comfortable position to rest. She looked up at the decorative light hanging from the ceiling before examining the rest of the room. Finally, her eyes landed on the plate of cookies next to the bed.

She reached for one, then the glass of milk. She took a tiny bite and thought her mouth was going to explode with pleasure! It was delicious! The milk, too, was incredibly good – not sour, as it often was by the time they got it at Winslow, but fresh and rich with butterfat. Tears sprang to her eyes as she sat there on the tiny bed, a cookie and a glass of milk in her hands, and realized she'd never had such a simple pleasure in her entire life.

Summer again looked to the ceiling above her head and whispered, "Thank You, Lord. Thank You for bringing me here. Please show me how to be a good wife to Mr. Riley, because I don't know the first thing about it."

She lowered her eyes and stared at the cookie in her hand. "But I can learn. I can learn everything I need to know to make a good wife. Please help me to do so!"

She didn't want to feel defeated. She'd made it this far, and was bound and determined to be the best spouse she could for Clayton Riley. But would her best be good enough?

She began to tick off a mental checklist of her gifts and talents. She could mend quite well, at least. The orphans at Winslow never had fine clothes, and were constantly tearing the threadbare ones they did have. She'd noticed how worn Clayton's shirts were in places – did he not have money enough to buy new ones, or had he just not bothered to fix them? She made a mental note of that too. She could, of course, keep a house clean; any idiot could do that. She knew how to cook a few simple dishes, like oatmeal and soup and sandwiches. An orphanage wasn't known for its fancy food, so she hadn't learned to make much else. Let's see, what else did a wife do …

Summer audibly gulped when she suddenly remembered *exactly* what else a wife did! *Oh, that!* Yes, well, she certainly didn't have any experience in that department. What if he was disappointed in her? She knew absolutely nothing of … of … and drat, *that* was certainly something she wouldn't be able to learn beforehand either!

She sighed, finished her cookie and milk, then laid her head against the pillow. In moments, sleep overcame her and she forgot all her worries and troubles for the time being. She hoped to dream of being a good wife, she wanted to dream of being someone special in Clayton Riley's eyes.

But instead, she had only nightmares.

SIX

Clayton heard a terrified scream from the study. Scratch that – it wasn't the study now, it was Summer's room ...

He threw the silverware onto the table he was setting and ran toward the sound, nearly knocking his mother off her feet as she came running from the kitchen. "I'll handle this," he told her before he burst into the room.

Miss James was sitting up in bed, her face bathed in sweat, her eyes wide as she shook with terror. Clayton didn't think at first, only reacted. "Miss James!" he said as he went to the bed and took her in his arms.

He instinctively scanned the room for anything amiss, but there was nothing. "What happened? We heard you scream," he said, his voice even, controlled. The lawman was back.

She looked up at him, tears in her eyes, then quickly turned her face away. Good Lord! What had she been dreaming? It was the only explanation. He certainly hoped whatever sort of nightmare she'd just had wasn't because of him! "It's ... it's nothing. I'm all right. I'm sorry if I disturbed you."

He tucked a finger under her chin and made her look at him again. "Nothing? That scream wasn't about nothing!" he told her firmly.

She tried to look away again but he held her fast. "Please," she began. "Just leave me be. I'll be fine."

He turned his head toward the door, where his mother was still standing. "Ma, I'll bring her to the supper table … but give us a few moments, will you?" Mrs. Riley looked them both over carefully before she nodded her agreement and left the room.

As soon as she was gone, Clayton turned back to the woman in his arms. "You know, if we're going to be man and wife, then you're going to have to talk to me about some things."

Her eyes, which had been glued to the desk beside the bed, slowly found their way to his. She swallowed hard, and he could not only see but felt the tension in her jaw. "Things?" she said in a low voice.

"Yep, things. Like why you left New Orleans in such a hurry. I may not be an expert at this mail-order bride business, but even I know that what you did had to have been done pretty quick-like."

She closed her eyes, and he could tell by the sudden pink of her cheeks she was hiding something. "Well?" He began in a soft voice. "Are you gonna tell me why you're so gosh darn scared right now?" Her eyes opened and she looked straight into his. There was such vulnerability harbored in them, hope and hopelessness mixed all together. What could have possibly happened to her? "Whatever it is," he added, "you don't have to be ashamed of it."

Her eyes widened.

"I understand that some women use a mail-order bride service because they're ... well, they're running from something. You ... you haven't gone and broken the law, now have ya? I'd hate to be the one to have to haul you in. How would that look to folks?"

Her face drained of color and her jaw was once again tight.

He'd better think of something fast. "Besides, no one wants to eat wedding cake in jail. I can hear the old biddies in town complaining already."

A tiny smile curved her mouth. Clayton stared at it a moment ... her sweet, delicious, little mouth. Now he had to swallow. Good Lord, but she was beautiful! It seemed as though every time he looked at her, he saw more and more of the beauty she possessed.

"It's ... not what you think," she said. "I haven't broken any laws."

"Well, that's good to hear." And he had to admit, he was glad she said it – though it wasn't enough to satisfy him, and he still planned to check a few things. For now, though, he wouldn't question her further. His mother was waiting for them, and Spencer would be coming in from the barn at any moment. But later they would finish this conversation, and he was going to find out what had happened to her if it was the last thing he did. He wasn't about to head into any sort of marriage until he got to the bottom of it. "You ready for supper, Miss James?"

She looked up at him and, without saying a word, nodded.

"All right, then, hang on to me."

She wrapped her arms around his neck. He smiled, overjoyed by the feeling of her holding him. Then he picked her up from the bed, stood and carried her into supper.

Summer sat in silence as the rest of the Riley family seated themselves around the table. Clayton said the blessing, and soon the meal was underway. No one spoke for a few moments as the food was passed and each of them served themselves.

She was a little surprised when Clayton, instead of passing the small platter of pot roast to her, served her himself. Then, without saying a word, he cut her meat for her as if it was the most natural thing for him to do. She watched as his brother Spencer did the same for their mother. She'd never seen such a thing, and had to consciously close her mouth when it threatened to hang open.

"Miss James," Mrs. Riley began. "Oh, but what am I doing calling you that – you're going to be my daughter-in-law, after all! Now, *Summer*, about your wedding dress. I understand you haven't one of your own."

"Ma, can't that wait?" Clayton was quick to interject. "She's in no shape for marrying yet."

"I know that, dear, but making a dress takes time, and we have to get started right away! By the time I'm done making it, her foot should be good enough to stand on."

Summer's eyes darted back and forth between mother and son.

"Abbey Davis will help." Spencer said between mouthfuls. "You know how she likes to sew all that fancy stuff."

"Yes, but her mother ... well ... you know she gives me a headache!" Mrs. Riley lamented. "I can't work like that – and besides, Abbey will talk poor Summer's ears off!"

Summer stopped chewing all together. She was hoping to be able to enjoy the meal (which was fabulous so far) and not have to talk, but it looked like that wasn't going to happen. She peeked sideways at Clayton, who looked like he was equally hoping to get through the meal in peace, but ...

"Ma ... please. No more talk of dresses, wedding cakes, or flowers while we're eating."

Mrs. Riley's eyes lit up. "Oh, I completely forgot about the cake! Why, thank you, Clayton. Be sure to stop by the Andersons' on your way to the jail tomorrow morning and see if Mrs. Anderson wouldn't mind handling the baking. She's so much better at decorating a cake than I am."

Clayton's mouth hung open as he looked at his mother. "Please?" was the only word to escape him before he took another bite of his dinner.

"But …" she began.

"No, Ma. I appreciate it, and I'm sure Miss James does too, but no more tonight. We've both had a tiring day. And besides, you should let Miss James decide on these things – it is her wedding after all, not to mention mine."

Summer chewed slowly. My, but the mashed potatoes were good. And the pot roast seemed to almost melt in her mouth! She'd never had anything so tasty at Winslow!

"Yes, I know that dear," Mrs. Riley began. "But I figured, what with her injury and all, that she wouldn't want to have to think about the details. I was just trying to help."

Summer took another bite of pot roast and continued to watch. Maybe if she was quiet enough, no one would actually talk *to* her – they'd just keep talking *about* her.

"I know, Ma. But … well, I don't think either of us are much up to talking about it right now. Besides, who knows when the wedding will be?"

Summer's chewing stopped as a chill went through her body. Had he changed his mind? Was he not going to set a date for their wedding because he thought she was lying to him about never being in trouble with the law?

"All right, Clayton, you win. I'll speak no more of it … tonight. But it does need to be discussed!" Mrs. Riley finished, her usual happy face transformed into one of disappointment. She looked around the table, then grumbled,

"Land sakes, at the rate you're moving, the two of you will be lucky to be wed by Christmas!"

Summer swallowed her food and watched the acute disappointment on Mrs. Riley's face as she took another bite of mashed potatoes. Perhaps the woman was right. Maybe she and Clayton wouldn't be married until Christmas. She suppressed a smile. She had long dreamed she would be married on Christmas Day! It was a silly thing, really – the fancy of a young child who used to wish for many things she knew would never happen. What were the chances?

But Christmas was over a month away. Surely her foot would be healed before then. Besides, if Mrs. Riley had her way, they'd be married the day after tomorrow with her injured foot propped on a chair! She wanted to marry Clayton – it was why she was there after all – and the thought of a Christmas wedding warmed her heart.

She sighed.

"Is something wrong, dear?" Mrs. Riley asked.

Summer looked up. All eyes were upon her. "Oh … why … no, everything's wonderful, Mrs. Riley. Thank you."

"Oh, I won't stand for being called Mrs. Riley," she admonished with a smile.

"Ma …" Clayton warned.

"Exactly, Clayton! Summer is going to be my daughter-in-law, and she might as well get used to calling me Ma, just as you two boys do!"

Another chill went up Summer's spine. He

didn't want her to call his mother "Ma"? Maybe he *was* planning on sending her back! Her stomach knotted with the thought.

"Ma!"

"Don't you sass me, young man! There is nothing wrong with Summer calling me that!"

Spencer let go a soft snicker from across the table.

"You shut up," Clayton warned.

"I wasn't going to say a thing!" Spencer said in his defense. "Besides, I agree with Ma."

"We're not married yet," Clayton grumbled as he stood up and left the table.

Summer trembled as cold seeped into her heart. At this rate, she'd be lucky if she got married at all. What was wrong with the man? Why was he tender at times, then suddenly cranky when their wedding was discussed?

"He'll be back," Spencer said. "Don't worry."

"Are … are you sure your brother wants to marry me?" Summer couldn't believe she'd asked it.

"Of course he wants to marry you!" Mrs. Riley quickly said. "He's just got cold feet – all prospective husbands do. That, and Clayton likes to be in control of things. He always wants everything just so, but I can teach you how to handle him. Just bake him up a pie or cake, and he'll be like putty in your hands!"

"He did have it rough while he was chasing those outlaws," Spencer told her. "It's hard to watch your men get shot up like the ones riding with Clayton did. He's worried about them too."

Summer took in his words. How would she feel if some of her fellow orphans had been harmed? How worried would she be? Would nuptials be the foremost thing on her mind? She didn't think so. She began to understand why Clayton was acting the way he was. Spencer was right – she needed to let him take care of business first and worry about the wedding details later.

Besides, there were more than wedding details on his mind. Of that Summer had no doubt – her true origins and what happened in New Orleans being foremost. How long would it be before he cornered her in her little room and asked … no… *demanded* to know? Of course, the right thing to do would be to tell him the truth. But what if he was disgusted by it? What would he think of a dirty orphan girl who had no choice but to marry him?

"Ma, where's the pie?" Clayton's voice yelled from the kitchen.

Spencer laughed and winked at Summer. "He always gets a sweet tooth when he's upset. Sure as the sun rising in the morning."

"Spence is right," Mrs. Riley told her as she reached across the table and patted her hand. "Clayton has had a rough few days. But as soon as he's had some dessert, he'll feel better."

Summer was about to comment when Clayton came back into the dining parlor with a pie in one hand, plates and a knife in the other. He laid everything out on the table, cut the pie and dished each of them up a slice. Mrs. Riley fetched a pot of coffee as he sat and began to dig in.

Summer did the same. The food in the Riley household was incredible, from the cookie she'd had that afternoon to the pot roast, potatoes, and apple pie that evening! Summer certainly hoped she'd be as good a cook as Mrs. Riley one day. Sure enough, the pie settled Clayton right down as if he'd been given some miracle elixir. She worried that if he ate her cooking, he'd go to the barn, saddle up his horse and head for the hills …

"Miss James, would you like to go out on the porch with me?"

Summer lifted her head, and found herself alone with Clayton at the table. She'd been so intent on her pie, and her thoughts, that she hadn't noticed Mrs. Riley and Spencer's departure. More than anything else, she wanted to be alone and think. But that wasn't about to happen – she needed to get this over with. "Of course," she replied as she took her last forkful.

Clayton got up from the table, scooped her up and left the dining parlor. He stopped near the front door, where his coat hung on a peg in the wall next to several others. "Here," he began as he managed to grab a shawl. "It's cold outside, and Ma won't mind if you wear this."

She took it from him, grateful. It was, of course, much colder here than in New Orleans, and she hadn't brought a decent coat with her. For that matter, she'd never owned a decent coat.

She clutched the shawl to her as he carefully opened the door with her in his arms and carried her outside. He nodded to a swing that hung at one end of the porch. It was a pretty thing, though functional and sturdy-looking. He sat her down, and she immediately wrapped the shawl around her shoulders. It was even colder than she thought it would be.

She started when he lowered himself down beside her, his weight making the swing sway to and fro. "Don't worry, it'll hold our weight. I built it myself."

"You did? It's very nice."

"Thank you." He cleared his throat, but said nothing more.

Summer pulled the shawl more tightly around herself before looking at him. He stared straight ahead, his eyes and face unmoving. But he wasn't looking *at* anything...

She glanced at her surroundings, not having had much time to take them in when she'd first arrived. The whole area was surrounded by trees – apple trees, judging by the few windfall fruit that speckled the ground. A large barn sat opposite the whitewashed farmhouse, and a chicken coop and several other outbuildings were also nearby. One looked like it might be a distillery, which made sense – they probably brewed their own apple cider.

She turned her face upward. The moon was bright, and the clear sky lit with stars. It was awe-inspiring. She'd never seen so many stars before – New Orleans had too many buildings in the way, and too many gas lamps blotting out their shine.

"They're pretty, aren't they?" Clayton asked

her. "I love these clear, cold nights."

She nodded as she looked at the stars beyond the barn. "Beautiful," she whispered.

"Yes, beautiful," he whispered in return.

She sensed his eyes on her but didn't look at him. Her heart began to thunder in her chest, and she couldn't figure out why. She finally concluded it was because he was going to question her about her past at any moment.

But that's not what Clayton Riley did. "I'm sorry, Miss James. I'm sorry for everything."

"What?"

"I shot you!" He shook his head. "No sooner than you got off the stage and I shot you. Then I left you at Doc and Milly's and let you think the worst of me. I should've made myself clearer on what I was doing. I should've sent word when I had to leave town with the posse … heck, I should've come and told you myself!"

"You've already apologized, Mr. Riley."

"Let me finish," he said as he put a finger against her lips to quiet her. His finger was warm despite the crisp chill in the air. For a scant second she wanted to kiss it as it lingered there, but he removed it before she could give in to the impulse.

"I'm not a trusting man by nature," he continued. "I guess that's one of the reasons I've survived being a lawman. You don't stay alive by assuming the best about folks. You stay alive by listening to what your gut tells you."

She stiffened. Here it comes …

"Miss James, what I'm trying to say is … well …"

"Mr. Riley, please … I can't go back."

He looked at her, eyebrows raised, mouth half-open. His eyes darted around before they settled on her once more. "Why not?"

She swallowed hard. "Bad things will happen if I do. I've nowhere to go."

"What about your family?"

"I …" She bit her lip. This was the moment she'd dreaded. "I don't have any family."

He furrowed his brow at her remark. "No family? Where are they?"

She shook her head and almost laughed. "I don't know."

He sat up straight and looked down at her like a horn just sprouted out of her head. "What do you mean, you don't know?"

"Mr. Riley, I don't know where my family is because I never had one to begin with."

She would *not* cry! To admit that no one wanted her, no one thought she was worth keeping, even adopting! She'd been rejected her whole life, and now he was going to do the same. He was going to ask it. She just knew he was going to ask the question she hated most of all!

"I don't understand. What happened?"

She looked him right in the eye. "Because, Mr. Riley. I'm an orphan."

SEVEN

"An orphan?" Clayton asked, his voice coming out an entire octave higher than normal. Summer James was an orphan? That explained a lot. He, on the other hand, had been about to admit he hadn't been the one to answer the advertisement for a mail-order bride – that his brother Spencer (and his accomplice, their mother) had sent in the request to the Ridgley Mail-Order Bride Company. But now this?

He caught the glisten of a single tear in the moonlight as it ran down one side of her face. He put a finger under her chin and pulled her face up to his. What he saw made his gut twist and his heart wrench. Shame. She had been horribly ashamed to tell him she was an orphan.

"How long have you been an orphan?" Perhaps it was a stupid question, but he wanted to know.

She sniffed. "All my life, for as far back as I can remember."

"You *never* knew your parents? That's plumb awful! I can't imagine what that must be like. So are you telling me you spent your entire life in an orphanage … until you turned eighteen?" He knew the law, of course; she would have to leave once she turned eighteen. But to spend her whole life in such a place, to never have been adopted … his stomach clenched tighter with the thought.

"Yes, but there was no work to be found, and … and …"

"And so you sought out the help of the mail-order bride service?"

She shook her head. "No, actually. They sought me out."

"Really?"

She nodded, "Yes – they contacted the orphanage. Mrs. Teeters, the headmistress, sent me there with a letter of recommendation that basically said I can read and write, knew my numbers, do at least a few things decently …" She almost choked at the admission.

Clayton's jaw clenched. *Noooo, not the tears!* But something stirred deep within him in that moment. Instead of running from the crying woman with his hackles up – which was his usual reaction in the company of a sobbing female – he instead sat up ramrod-straight. The action was pronounced enough to make the swing move. His jaw tightened and his eyes narrowed as a wave of fierce protectiveness washed over him. How could this happen? How could a beautiful woman such as this go unnoticed as a child, spending her entire life without being adopted by a set of loving parents? It was one of life's many cruelties, and he hated it. As a lawman he'd seen far too much cruelty toward people, especially women.

His hands balled into fists for a moment before he forcibly relaxed them, took her in his arms and held her close. "I'm sorry Miss James. I'm sorry you've never had anyone to belong to. I can't imagine, can't begin to fathom …"

She trembled in his arms.

Clayton now understood her panicked display in town, what caused her to fall into such hysterics. It was like the icing on the proverbial cake of rejection. To finally think that for once in your life you were going to belong somewhere, to someone, only to suddenly have it look like you would be sent back … he shut his eyes tight against the discovery that he'd caused the woman in his arms such anguish. Worse yet, he hadn't even realized he had until he and Spencer were bringing her back to the farm.

"There now, don't cry. You're safe here, understand?" And, he suddenly realized, she was. How could he possibly think of sending her back when he knew what she'd endured? Of course he would marry her, and one day (he hoped) they would come to love each other. But that could take time; Sarah's death had left a hole in his heart the size of Texas, and he wasn't sure anyone could fill it. But at least the woman in his arms would provide him with some company and fill the lonely nights in his bed.

"I … I'm sorry I'm being such a ninny. I don't usually cry so much, it's just that …"

"You don't need to explain yourself, honey. You've been through more than anyone should.

I'm glad you told me. It helps me make more sense of things." He held her away from him and looked at her. Even with tear-filled eyes and a nose red from cold and crying, she looked adorable in the moonlight. "Tomorrow, you and Ma talk wedding details while I'm working. I'll give her some money, and when you're up to it, the two of you can go into town and get what you need."

She smiled at him like a child who'd just been given the best Christmas present in the world. "Oh, thank you, Mr. Riley! Thank you!"

He gathered her into his arms again and held her close. He was going to have to get her out of the cold and into the house, but he couldn't resist holding her a few minutes more. She fit into his embrace like a glove, and he liked the feel of her small body wrapped in his strong arms. How he'd missed this! What had he been thinking all these years, denying himself the company of a woman? Sarah was gone, and like it or not, she wasn't coming back. Waiting all this time had done nothing but make him even lonelier, and more bitter.

But the woman in his arms was beginning to melt the winter in his heart. How aptly named she was – Summer! Summertime to his cold, barren, wasteland of a life.

Of course, none of it meant Spencer wasn't going to get the licking of his life! Clayton still wanted to kill him, if only for pride's sake. He inwardly chuckled at the thought before giving the woman in his arms a healthy squeeze. "There now, sugar, you just let me take care of everything. Before you know it, you'll be up and around, and we'll be married."

"Thank you again, Mr. Riley!" she mumbled into his chest.

He smiled. "Don't you think it's time you started calling me by my Christian name?"

She sniffed back more tears and looked up at him. "Thank you … Clayton."

He smiled again as he looked down at her and wiped some of her tears away with a finger. "What was I thinking all these years?"

"I beg your pardon?" she said between little hiccups.

He shook his head. "Nothing to concern yourself with, honey. Suffice to say I can be stubborn at times, not to mention stupid. You might as well know that about me."

She wiped at what tears remained with the back of her hand. "I'm sure there's a lot for us to learn about each other, especially since we never got the chance to write one another beforehand."

He stiffened slightly. "Ah, yes. Very true." He took a deep breath, prepared to tell her the reason for the lack of correspondence … and couldn't do it. "I'd … best get you back inside before you freeze to death." He glanced at the sky beyond the porch and noticed the clouds rolling in. "I'll bet it snows later tonight."

"Do you get much snow here?"

"Depends. Every year is a little different."

"Do … do you get snow at Christmastime?" Her voice was hopeful, childlike.

It made the protectiveness within him

double. He had to take another deep breath to steady himself. "Sometimes. I bet it does this year."

"I've always wanted to see a white Christmas. To decorate a beautiful tree … to have presents to wrap and give."

Good God, how much had she gone without, growing up an orphan? Clayton Riley made a vow to himself right then and there – he was going to make sure he gave Summer James the best Christmas she'd ever had! "You concentrate on healing up, and I'll see about the rest, all right?"

She looked up into his eyes, her face locked in shock. He knew right there that she'd never had the things he did growing up. Sure, the orphanage would have had some kind of Christmas holiday. But a poor one might only have a little extra food for Christmas dinner, nothing more...

He cupped her face with one large hand. "I'll see to everything, you hear? Don't you worry your pretty little head about a thing. This will be the best Christmas you've ever had."

A few tears escaped again, tears that for once made Clayton smile. For these were tears of relief and pure joy.

And it felt good, he found. Real good.

Summer relaxed against him as he picked her up from the swing and carried her into the warm embrace of the house. The smell of apple pie and coffee hung in the air, and she thought she'd never smelled anything so wonderful – except for the dinner that had preceded it! In fact, she felt so relieved she had trouble keeping her tears of joy at bay. Every time she thought about what Clayton had said, that they would be married soon and that she needn't worry about a thing, well … it was almost too good to be true! At last she would belong somewhere, and have a family to call her own, even a mother! And though she had yet to really get to know the Rileys, she was sure she would come to love them all very quickly.

Especially Clayton. She could fall in love with him quite easily, especially now that there was no doubt in her mind they would be wed! How wonderful, how blissful her life had suddenly become! She never dreamed anything like it could ever happen to her.

But what of the others? All her friends at Winslow that she'd left behind … many of them were approaching eighteen as well. What would become of them?

Summer sobered at the thought as Clayton carried her into her small room and set her down upon the bed. "Ma will be in to help you get ready for bed and see to anything you might need. I'll be long gone by the time you get up, but I'll see you come suppertime."

She looked up at him, "Thank you. Thank you again – for everything."

He cupped her face with his hand. "You don't have to thank me – you should be thanking ..." He suddenly froze, as his nerve failed him again.

"Who? I don't understand?"

He smiled and coughed into one hand. "Um, well ... shucks, never mind me – I don't know what I'm talking about. It's been a long day, and tomorrow's gonna be even longer. You get some sleep now, honey, and I'll see you tomorrow night." He winked at her as he left the room.

The word "honey" stood out as if it hung in the air with the apple pie and coffee aroma. She liked the endearment, and it made her heart flutter every time he'd said it that evening, despite her being so upset at times.

Summer chastised herself for not having faith in the good Lord's decision-making where her life was concerned. Truly He knew what He was doing sending her to Nowhere, and she was sure He wasn't done with her yet. But she also realized that so far she hadn't been very good at trusting the Almighty with her life's details, and figured she'd better get a hold of herself and make good with Him. She clasped her hands together quickly and sent up a prayer that she'd do just that.

Mrs. Riley burst into the room. "Oh, my sweet dear, Clayton just gave me the news! We'll start planning first thing in the morning! Of course, this means I'll need to round up some help – it's too big an undertaking for one person! Oh, Nellie Davis will be just green with envy that my Clayton is getting married! She's had her eye on Clayton for her daughter

Charlotte since he was knee-high to a grasshopper!"

Summer sat in stunned silence. Did the woman ever breathe?

Mrs. Riley prattled on about wedding details as she busied about the room, pulling a nightgown from a trunk at the end of the bed. She helped Summer into it as she continued to talk non-stop. By the time Summer was ready and Mrs. Riley blew out the lamp on the desk, Summer thought she might explode from holding the laughter in.

But some of the things Mrs. Riley had talked about gave her pause, and her thoughts lingered on them as she stared at the moonlight streaming in through the window. Who was this Charlotte Davis? Why hadn't Clayton married her if Mrs. Davis was so adamant about it? Mrs. Riley made it sound like, had Summer not come along when she did, he would have been doomed to marry Charlotte and spend the rest of his days in dismal servitude to the woman. The thought was almost laughable. She couldn't picture Sheriff Clayton Riley being in any sort of servitude to anyone, let alone a woman. Surely Charlotte Davis couldn't be *that* bad? Could she?

And what of her mother? Mrs. Riley painted her as some busybody wicked witch that wanted nothing more than to marry both her daughters to both of *her* sons. And even though Mrs. Riley spoke well of Abbey, the younger daughter, she and Spencer had never hit it off. They were good friends, yes, but had no attraction for one another as far as Mrs. Riley could see. Without love, what sort of marriage would they have?

And that was the most troubling thought of all. She and Clayton themselves were going into a marriage without love, or even friendship – neither had had the time to form. Would they be able to build a lasting union? Or would they simply be two people who shared a house, meals and a bed? And did it really matter? It still meant she'd have a decent life, away from the poverty of the orphanage, from the horrible streets of New Orleans and men like Mr. Slade.

Summer sent up another quick prayer that the other girls at Winslow would be delivered from the same fate. Marriage as a mail-order bride was far better than the misery waiting to swallow them up the moment they set foot from outside its doors.

Her thoughts stilled and her eyes widened as she noticed some movement outside the window.

She suddenly sat up and stared in awe at the sight of snow, gently falling through the fading streams of moonlight. Clouds began to blot out the stars as they slowly moved across the sky to settle in and send to earth what would surely blanket the farm with beautiful white by morning.

Snow! She had never seen it, not even during her long journey to Nowhere. Oh, sure, it was evident in the mountains above the cities and towns she'd passed through on her way. She'd stared at the snow-covered hills for as long as she could as the stagecoach rumbled along, until they'd been blocked by other sights or she'd gotten a kink in her neck. There was more sunshine than anything else once the stage entered Washington Territory, and she began to wonder at the stories she'd heard from her fellow passengers about the never-ending rain that supposedly plagued this part of the country. But she wasn't going all the way to Oregon City – Nowhere was at least three hundred miles northeast of there. The sun was obviously much more abundant in this part of the territory, and for that she was glad.

She settled back as best she could without moving her foot too much, put her hands behind her head and sighed in contentment. Snow … pure, clean and bright. To Summer, it represented the beginning of her new life. And it was all due to God, Mrs. Ridgley and Mrs. Teeters. And the Rileys, of course.

She smiled, prayed for all her benefactors, closed her eyes, and for the first time in as long as she could remember, fell into a blissful, dream-filled sleep.

EIGHT

The next day passed pleasantly. As Clayton had promised, Summer didn't see him until suppertime, neither him nor his brother. Their mother took advantage of the absent menfolk to see to it Summer got cleaned up.

In the afternoon, Mrs. Riley helped her into a chair and washed her hair over a small metal tub on the floor, using a bucket of hot water and a pitcher for rinsing. Then she helped her wash her body as best she could, seeing as she was unable to get into a tub herself.

Summer was used to this type of "dry bathing," as there was never enough time – or water – for an actual bath at the orphanage. The place had several tubs, but they usually had multiple children in each, and she and the older orphans had had to help Mrs. Teeters take care of the endless stream of dirty little ones before they could see to their own hygiene.

But she'd never had anything like Mrs. Riley's next surprise. The woman presented her with a beautiful dark-red dress she had stored in the attic. "It was mine when I was your age. It certainly doesn't fit me anymore, but I think it should fit you. I wish I had another for you to have for day use, but I gave them all away. I saved this one, though."

"Why did you save it?"

Mrs. Riley smiled as she held the dress up. "I was wearing it the day I met my dear Charles. It was Christmastime, and I was singing in the church Christmas pageant. That was when Charles and I both lived in Philadelphia. Oh, those were grand days! I should bring the hat down too – it matches the dress perfectly! I don't know what happened to my red jacket or muffler, but I'm sure we can order something similar at the mercantile."

"Oh, Mrs. Riley, it's so beautiful! If I can get some yarn and knitting needles, I can probably knit a shawl. You don't have to go through all the trouble and expense of buying a coat and muffler."

"Nonsense, child! You'll freeze to death out here once winter really sets in! And besides, you can't have a good old-fashioned snow fight with the boys wearing just a shawl!"

"Snow fight?"

"Yes, dear, it's tradition! My cousins travel here every year and spend the holidays with us. With luck we'll have snow, and then you'll see a real free-for-all! But even if there isn't any snow, they'll be excited all the same because of your wedding!"

A tingle of delight raced up Summer's spine. Mrs. Riley hadn't been able to stop talking about wedding details for more than two minutes the entire day.

"Now lean on me, dear, and brace yourself while I smooth out the skirt."

Summer did as instructed, standing on one foot and holding onto one of Mrs. Riley's shoulders while she bent over and brushed out the skirt with her hands. "How do I look?" she asked when the woman finally stood.

Mrs. Riley brought a chair over. "Hang onto this, dear," she said as she walked a circle around her and inspected her handiwork. "Oh, it's beautiful! A little outdated maybe, but you're as pretty as a picture! Wait until Clayton gets a gander at you! Won't he be fit to be tied?"

"Fit … to be tied?" Summer echoed, worry in her voice.

"Oh don't misunderstand me – I mean he's gonna bust a gut he'll be so enamored with how you look! I bet he starts thinking about running into town to fetch the preacher straightaway!"

Summer relaxed. Her insecurity at the unfamiliar remark surprised even her. She had to learn to trust the Rileys and take them at their word. Of course, she also needed to be sure she understood clearly whatever words came out of their mouths, or she might have another misunderstanding like the one with Clayton the day before. She certainly didn't want a repeat of *that*!

Summer was in bed, reading from a book of poetry while Mrs. Riley – having settled her back in – went about preparing supper. But she'd no sooner started the fourth poem when she heard voices and the sound of horses trotting into the barnyard. The brothers must be home.

She sat up straighter and craned her neck to see out the window, but her little room was on the wrong side of the house and she couldn't see the barnyard. What she could see was the remains of the beautiful dusting of snow she'd awoken to that morning. She hoped it would snow again. She longed to touch it, feel it against her skin, even taste it! What she'd really like to do was lay in it and make snow angels like the ones she heard Elnora talk about. She sighed in remembrance as she listened to the Riley brothers' voices drift in through the glass of her window.

Elnora … how she missed her friend. Elle was always getting into trouble. She could still hear Mrs. Teeters yelling, *Elnora Barstow! Your parents are gonna turn over in their graves when they see what you're doing!* She and Elle would giggle, then run like the dickens to avoid getting caught by Mrs. Teeters or her handyman Clarence for their mischief. What fun it had been!

Summer wondered what Elle was going to do when it came her time to leave. Good heavens, that could be any day now! Her birthday was … she quickly calculated dates in her head … good Lord! Elle's birthday was next week! "Oh, no."

"Oh, no what?" Clayton asked from the

doorway.

Summer jumped. She'd been so busy trying to figure out Elle's birthday that she hadn't heard him enter the house. "Lord have mercy, you scared me!"

"I could see that – you about came off the bed. Now ... *oh, no* what?"

Summer blinked at him a few times as she tried to gather her wits. "My ... my friend Elle. Elnora Barstow, actually – Elle's her nickname. Her birthday is next week."

"Are you worried she'll think you forgot?" Clayton asked as he pulled the chair away from the desk and sat.

"No, no, it's not that. It's ..."

He looked her over carefully as he took in her expression. "It's ... what?"

"Nothing," she said quickly.

"That nothing means something, Miss James. And I aim to find out what."

Summer gulped. She could see she wouldn't be able to keep secrets from Sheriff Clayton Riley. It was probably one of the things that had made him a sheriff in the first place. "She ... she's turning eighteen."

Clayton rubbed his chin with his hand a few times before he looked at her. "I see. And that means she's about to be in the same pickle that you were in, is that it?"

Summer nodded. The thought of Mr. Slade getting his vile hands on Elle made her entire body go cold. "If she can't find work right away ..."

"She has just as good a chance as you did.

Besides, maybe she'll become a mail-order bride as well – and if she's lucky, land herself a fellow as handsome as me."

She smiled and her shoulders shook with silent mirth. But his teasing didn't make the cold, dark feeling of dread go away, and Summer began to wonder how she might get in touch with her friend ...

"My, don't you look pretty!" Clayton suddenly exclaimed, distracting her from her train of thought. "That color looks incredible on you! What a beautiful shade of red! Wherever did you ... oh, is that ...?"

Summer blushed from head to toe at his compliments. "Yes, it's your mother's," she said as his brow knit together in recollection. Surely he'd seen the dress before, but his expression clearly told her he hadn't been totally sure where or when.

"Of course – I remember seeing it up in the attic! You mean to tell me my mother dragged that old thing out of a trunk and put you in it?"

"But you just said it was beautiful!"

"I did, and it is." He sat up straight. "But no wife of mine is going to wear hand-me-downs."

Summer practically melted when he said it. It wasn't just the look on his face, decisive and determined, that had that effect. It was that one word – *wife*. She reveled in it when it escaped his lips.

"But enough of all that, I'm starved. How about you?"

She smiled, nodded, and let Clayton scoop her up into his arms so he could carry her into the dining parlor. He turned toward the door with her and stopped.

"What is it?" she asked.

He stood and thought a moment, opened his mouth to speak, then shut it again. Finally he looked down at her, his eyes softened with a tenderness she'd not seen before. "I think I'm gonna miss this once your foot heals."

Summer blushed a bright pink and smiled shyly back.

Clayton readjusted her in his arms, grinned, and took her in to supper.

The next day, company arrived, and Mrs. Riley was abuzz with nervous chatter at the untimely and unexpected intrusion. "Oh, dear! It's that Nellie Davis and her daughter Charlotte!" she exclaimed the minute she saw the buggy pull up outside. "How rude to just drop in unannounced! Here to check out the competition, no doubt!"

"Competition?"

Mrs. Riley turned to her from her place at the parlor window. She'd helped Summer hop into the room after breakfast, after Summer asked to spend the day someplace, *anyplace* other than the tiny bedroom. She wasn't used to being idle, and certainly couldn't stand to just sit by herself all day. She wanted to make herself useful, and had offered to do some of the mending. Mrs. Riley had happily agreed, but no sooner had they gotten settled with patches and thread than the Davis women had driven their buggy into the barnyard.

"Yes, competition. And let me assure you, my dear, that's just how they see you! If I've told Nellie once, I've told her a thousand times that Clayton won't have anything to do with Charlotte, but the woman won't listen! Maybe after she sees you, she'll give up and leave us be!" She let the lace curtains fall back into place, then wrung her hands together. "I guess there's no help for it. We'll just have to muddle through the visit as best we can. I do wish Abbey had come with them – she, at least, would soften the blows."

"Mrs. Riley, are they really that bad?"

Her usual happy expression turned to a frown. "Yes," she stated flatly, then said, "Brace yourself, dear; they shoot with both barrels."

Summer's mouth dropped open at the comment. For heaven's sake, if the women were *that* bad, then why were they allowed into the house in the first place?

A loud knock sounded at the door and Summer straightened in her chair. She almost wished she was wearing Mrs. Riley's beautiful red evening dress, but it wasn't appropriate for day use. Instead she wore her old dress from the orphanage, the one she'd had in her satchel. She'd figured it was good as anything to sit around and convalesce in. Of course, that was when she wasn't expecting to deal with visitors. At least her face was clean and her hair was up.

She took a deep breath as Mrs. Riley

answered the front door.

A shrill voice came from the hall. "Why, Leona Riley! We had no idea you'd be home! I thought for sure you'd be in town shopping for the wedding!" Summer couldn't see the front door from where she sat, but cringed at the remark nonetheless. The accent was one she recognized from New Orleans – that of a high-cotton, plantation-bred Southern belle. The type who would sooner cross the street than let the perfumed air around her be corrupted by a poor orphan. And, in Summer's experience, did.

"If you thought I was in town, then what in heaven's name are you doing here, Nellie?"

A different voice chimed in, with the same drawl but younger and oilier. "Oh, Mother and I brought your guest something to make her feel better. I baked them myself." *The infamous Charlotte.* A pang of jealousy pierced Summer's heart and she quickly pushed it away. How could she be jealous of a woman whom Clayton supposedly had nothing to do with?

Supposedly...

The women glided into the room with tiny, precise steps, Mrs. Riley right behind them, her frown firmly in place as she eyed the two with suspicion. Summer felt her spine stiffen in the chair.

"Oh, there you are! Aren't you just a vision!" Charlotte exclaimed. "Look, Mother, isn't she just too adorable with her foot all wrapped in bandages like that? Kind of reminds me of our milk cow Effie when she broke her leg." She turned to Summer. "We had to shoot her, of course, to put her out of her misery." Her face suddenly took on a wide-eyed look of innocence. "Does it pain you something awful, dear? Oh, my! And to think we can't take you out and put you out of your misery like poor Effie! I'm afraid you'll just have to suffer through!"

Oh. My. Lord, Summer thought. She chanced a glance at Mrs. Riley, who looked as if lightning was about to shoot out of her eyes to obliterate the two women. Summer clamped her mouth tightly shut to keep from laughing.

Nellie turned to Mrs. Riley, whose suspicious look immediately sweetened into a smile. "I declare, Leona, hasn't the child anything decent to wear? Just look at that old rag she's got on! Aren't you the least bit embarrassed?"

Summer's spine stiffened further. She couldn't help it if what she wore was all she had. She could see that Mrs. Riley wholeheartedly agreed – her eyes still looked like they could be lethal weapons.

"Miss James and I are going into town to purchase what we need for a new wardrobe, just as soon as she's up to it. *Clayton* would have it no other way."

Summer immediately noticed Charlotte's jaw clench. *Direct hit.* The girl turned to her mother, her brow raised in question. "And would this mean you're going to see Mrs. Jorgensen?"

"Of course it does! What other dressmaker is there in town?" Mrs. Riley asked firmly.

Charlotte slowly turned back to face Summer. "I see. Well, you'll certainly be pleased with Mrs. Jorgensen's work. She used to be a dressmaker in Boston before coming out West. Why she bothers with any of the scruff in this town, I simply don't know."

Summer's eyes narrowed. Charlotte was trying to make going to the dressmaker sound like it was for the underprivileged, but even Summer knew better.

Nellie took a step toward her and looked her up and down like she was a trinket in a shop – or thrown out the back door of one. "Obviously, she'll suit you better than your last dressmaker."

Charlotte giggled. "Oh, Mother, you are a card! It's quite apparent she's never seen a dressmaker in her life! Have you, sweet thing?"

Summer's hands clutched the arms of the chair. "I never had to. I make my own clothes."

Nellie smirked. "Then perhaps Leona can give you a few sewing lessons to correct an area in which you're sadly lacking. I must say, Leona, she's more homely than I thought." She turned to Mrs. Riley with an air of innocence.

"Nellie Davis, how dare you come into my home and insult my son's future bride!" Mrs. Riley spat.

Nellie closed the distance between herself and the chair in which Summer sat. "Well, look at her! I mean, really – the idea of a fine man like Clayton marrying the likes of this! Surely you've lost your senses! She's so thin, for one thing!"

"I don't like the look of her eyes," Charlotte commented nonchalantly. "They look dull. If she doesn't get some decent rest, everyone will think she's stupid."

Summer's eyes widened as her mouth tightened in anger. She barely managed to quell the burning retort she had at the ready. One didn't spend life in an orphanage and not know how to fight back. It was full of children from the streets and surrounding swamplands. Some children came to the orphanage and acted little better than animals.

But then, one also didn't spend life in an orphanage and not know *when* to fight back. And perhaps in this case, discretion was the better part of valor ...

Mrs. Davis smirked. "Leona, doesn't she know she's in polite company? Is the poor child dumb?"

Or was it? Summer glanced about the room. "Of course not," she calmly said. "It's just that I find your company to be so ..." She made a show of looking Mrs. Davis and her daughter up and down as they had done to her. "... *interesting.*"

Charlotte's eyes flashed along with her mother's as they realized Summer was a worthy opponent. Mrs. Davis quickly turned to Mrs. Riley. "Do let us know if you need help with the wedding preparations. That is ... well ..." She stepped over to her and whispered – but loud enough so Summer could hear every word. "... if Clayton is *really* serious about marrying this girl. After all, she's obviously lacking – and you know our Clayton only deserves the best. But men can be so stubborn when it comes to admitting they've made a mistake. I'm sure sending her back won't be too much trouble. You'll let me know if you need help with that, won't you?"

Mrs. Riley's eyes narrowed to slits. "Summer is not going anywhere. Clayton fully intends to marry her, Nellie Davis, so you might as well give it up!"

Mrs. Davis's hand flew to her chest in shock. "Why, Leona! My dear sweet friend, whatever do you mean?"

Before Mrs. Riley had a chance to comment (or possibly shriek, as her face was turning redder by the second), Charlotte grabbed her mother by the arm and steered her toward the front hall. "Obviously the whole family is as stubborn and as proud as Clayton, Mother. But rest assured, they'll figure out the error of their ways and come to their senses. All we can do in the meantime is pray." Her face had taken on the most angelic look Summer had ever seen. Her own face twisted up at the brazenness of the girl – she didn't know whether to laugh or just sit there and stare in utter shock. Thankfully, her injured foot eliminated the possibility of getting up and slapping the silly twerp ... though she was tempted to try anyway.

"Well, I must say, Leona, I never thought I'd see the day you'd let your son marry a woman he's only just met. And to think she came through the mail, no less!"

"It was by train and stagecoach, actually," Summer replied dryly.

"Whatever," Mrs. Davis said as she dismissed the comment with a wave of her hand. "Well, I'll not stand here any longer and see you taken in by this charade. I'll do whatever I can to help you. You just let me know when you want to get her out of your house!"

"She's not going anywhere, Nellie. She's going to marry Clayton."

"Ohhhh, I just can't stand it!" Charlotte wailed. "What will people in town think of our sheriff marrying such a dull girl?"

At that, Summer lost her patience. "Oh, for heaven's sake!" She rolled her eyes, then looked to Mrs. Riley. "Are they always like this?"

"Oh, no, dear. Not this bad, but still …"

"Well! Of all the nerve, Leona! And I thought you were my friend!" Mrs. Davis huffed. "Come, Charlotte, we don't have to take this sort of ill treatment!" The two women stomped to the front door, threw it open and stormed out into the cold sunshine.

Mrs. Riley's shoulders drooped after the dramatic exit. She slowly made her way to the door and closed it, re-entered the parlor and plopped into a chair next to Summer. "I'm afraid there will be no peace for us now."

"What do you mean? I've dealt with people like that before."

"Oh, my dear," she said as she reached over and patted her on the leg. "Maybe you've dealt with the type – but you haven't dealt with Nellie Davis. She's a spiteful thing, and she's never gotten over Clayton rejecting Charlotte. As long as I can remember she's counted on Clayton and Charlotte getting married. Too bad she never once informed Clayton of the fact."

"What?" Summer said in shock. "You mean she literally planned it all out and then expected it to happen?"

Mrs. Riley nodded. "Something like that. Now with you here, she's going to be exceptionally nasty to deal with. I've never seen either one of them *this* bent out of shape before. Apparently she's still holding out for her plan to come to fruition."

"What sort of person does such a thing?" Summer asked, truly perplexed.

Mrs. Riley grimaced. "Nellie Davis."

"But why do you put up with her? Why even let her set foot in your house?"

Mrs. Riley let go a long sigh. "Because … she wasn't always like this. Long ago when we were both young, we really were the best of friends."

Summer shifted in her chair and automatically leaned toward the older woman. "What happened?"

Mrs. Riley calmly shrugged. "The thing that usually happens to split best friends apart. A man."

NINE

Clayton pinned the wanted poster up on the wall, then stepped back and took a good look at it. Had he ever seen the man? He didn't think so, but for some reason "Red Ned" looked awfully familiar.

"That's a nice reward for Ned." Spencer remarked.

"Sure wish I could remember where I've seen him."

"He does look kind of familiar, doesn't he?" Spencer said as he peered at the likeness of the bearded, one-eyed man. "Shouldn't be too hard to spot. Just look for a man with an eye patch!"

"Could be other ways to hide a missing eye. He might have a fake one. Be sure to tell the boys to keep an eye out–"

Spencer burst out laughing.

"No pun intended," Clayton chuckled. "But seriously, he was spotted down near Clear Creek a few months ago, then again about fifty miles southeast of here."

"Think he has anything to do with that outlaw gang we've been after lately?"

"Don't know. All I know is, it's lunchtime. Let's go down to Hank's and get something."

"Sure," Spencer agreed as he went for his hat.

Billy Blake, Clayton's other deputy, sauntered into the office from the cell area. "Where ya goin', boss?"

"Lunch," Clayton answered. "You want us to bring you back something?"

"Nah – Abbey Davis is bringing me mine," Billy drawled with a smile.

"Abbey Davis!" Spencer said, surprised. "Since when did you and Abbey start courting?"

Billy smiled and winked. "Just now. Done run into the pretty little thing this mornin' as she was walkin' into town. I was takin' my daddy's wagon to leave at the livery – springs need fixin'. Poor lil' gal was freezin', so I done drove 'er the rest of the way."

"Why was Abbey walking? What's wrong with their rig?" Clayton asked.

"On account her sister Charlotte and their ma went out to pay a visit to yer place."

Clayton was about to put on his hat, but froze with it halfway to his head. "*Our* place?"

"Yep, Abbey done said she wanted to go too – said she was lookin' forward to meetin' yer bride-to-be. But her ma made 'er come into town and get some things at the mercantile. I told Mr. Quinn to make sure she got home all right, an' he said he'd leave Mrs. Quinn to mind the store and drive 'er home hisself. Abbey told me she'd come by here with somethin' to show her 'preciation 'fore Mr. Quinn left with her."

Spencer grinned. "You gonna hold out for a kiss?"

"Spencer!" Clayton snapped. "Never mind about that. Mrs. Davis and Charlotte went to the house this morning!"

"Are you worried there may have been bloodshed? Maiming, maybe?"

Clayton glared at his brother. "Nothing that extreme, but you know how Mrs. Davis and Ma get when it comes to …"

"… your bachelorhood – which, of course, is about to be remedied," Spencer finished for him.

"I'm probably overreacting. I'm sure the visit was fine …"

Before anyone could speak, the door of the sheriff's office opened and Charlotte Davis walked in.

"… or not." Clayton put on his hat and turned toward the door, cringing already.

Charlotte sashayed her way to where he stood. "Why, Clayton!" she exclaimed. "I'm so glad I caught you – I must speak with you immediately!"

Clayton sighed and glanced to Spencer, who stood with an innocent smirk on his face. "I'll catch up with you later, Spence. Order my usual for me, will you?"

Spencer nodded, tipped his hat to Charlotte, and left.

"Billy, do you mind?" Charlotte asked. "I'd like to speak with Clayton in *private*."

Billy shrugged and left to wait for Abbey outside. As soon as he was gone, Charlotte spun on Clayton. "Oh, Clayton! I'm so *very* sorry!"

Clayton raised a curious brow and crossed him arms. "Sorry for what?"

"I didn't want to be the one to tell you this, but I just can't stand by and stay quiet any longer!"

When could you stay quiet ever? Clayton thought. He tipped back his hat and sighed. "Quiet about what, Charlotte?"

She pressed her lips together a moment as if the dread of her next words was almost too much for her to bear. "That woman, the one in your house? She's a criminal!"

"What?" Clayton replied, already suspicious.

Charlotte's eyes grew round as saucers. "It's true! I swear it! She ... she ..."

Clayton narrowed his eyes. "She what?"

"She's just using this whole mail-order bride business because ... because she's running from the law!"

He sighed again. "Charlotte, in all my years of knowing you, I never thought I'd see the day when you would sink–"

"Clayton Riley, you can't marry that horrible creature! She'll plumb ruin you! She's lied to you from the start!"

Clayton uncrossed his arms, but only to massage his forehead. Maybe if he rubbed hard enough, the headache she was causing would stop before it really got going. Or better yet, maybe *she* would stop ...

Unfortunately, his ministrations were interrupted when she threw her arms around his neck. "Can't you see it, Clayton? She's running

from the law and if you marry her it will only
get you into a heap of trouble!"

"Charlotte, I'm sorry you're so upset about
this, but what's done is done."

She immediately stilled. "What do you
mean?"

He gently removed her arms from his person.
"I am going to marry Miss James. It doesn't
matter who sent for her – I'm marrying her."

Her eyes widened. "You mean you're not the
one who sent away for a mail-order bride?" she
squeaked.

He slowly shook his head. Maybe if she
knew that Spencer sent for Miss James and that
Clayton planned to marry her anyway, Charlotte
would finally, *finally* give up the notion he'd
marry *her*. "Spencer answered the advertisement
for a mail-order bride, not me. But his intention
was to send away for one *for* me."

Now Charlotte began to rub her own
forehead. "Wait a minute! You mean to tell me
your brother sent away for a bride so *you* could
get married?"

He nodded. "Yes. And I must say, he chose
well."

Her face ran through a series of shocked
expressions before finally settling between rage
and heartbreak. For a moment he regretted
telling her, but it did look like it was having the
desired effect. "You … you'd marry a complete
stranger that you didn't even send for … over
me?"

Clayton took a deep breath. "Charlotte,
we've been over this a hundred times. You're a

well-bred girl, and I'm sure you'll make some fellow a fine wife, but I don't fancy you that way. My heart simply does not lead me in that direction. How cruel would I be to marry you when I know I don't love you?"

She pressed her lips together again. Her hands balled into fists at her sides, her body shaking now from her barely controlled rage. "I see. I see that I'm not good enough for you, Clayton Riley. That you'd rather marry some little gutter tramp that you know nothing about than me! How much love is in that?"

"Well, I wouldn't quite put it that way …"

"No!" Charlotte held up a hand as if to stop him. "You don't have to say anything else. I understand."

Clayton looked at her doubtfully. "You do?"

"Yes. I can't help it if you've lowered your standards. Go ahead, marry the girl. I wish you both the best."

"That's mighty kind of you, Charlotte," he replied, ignoring her obvious insult. "Thank you."

"But tell me, Clayton. If Spencer hadn't sent away for a *mail-order bride*, would you have given marriage a second thought? Would anything else have changed?"

"I suppose it took meeting Miss James to wake me up a little and realize I needed to move on."

"So now that you realize it, you're ready to marry?"

He thought on it a moment, then nodded. "Yes. Yes, I am."

She made a show of smoothing her skirt and adjusting her bonnet. "Well, bless you both, then." She held out her hand.

Clayton stared at it a second before he finally took it. She made to shake, but he instead bent at the waist, raised her hand to his lips and kissed it. "Thank you, Charlotte. I knew you'd understand."

"Well, I guess the best woman won." She didn't sound like she meant it.

"Don't take it too hard. Your man will come along someday."

"Yes, I suppose," she pouted. "I just wish he'd hurry it up. He takes any longer and I'll be nothing but an old maid."

Clayton smiled and let go her hand. "Never."

The door to the sheriff's office opened and Charlotte's sister Abbey stood in the doorway. "Charlotte, there you are! What are you and Mother doing in town? I thought you'd still be visiting out at the Riley farm."

"No, Mother needed to speak with Mrs. Jorgensen. I suppose you can ride home with us now that you're here." She turned without looking at Clayton and headed for the door. Billy moved out of the way as she sashayed past and went out onto the boardwalk. "Come along, Abbey. Mother's waiting, I'm sure."

Abbey nodded to Clayton, gave Billy a bright smile, then followed her sister off the boardwalk and across the street.

Clayton and Billy watched the sisters as they walked away, their skirts swishing to and fro as then went. "That Abbey Davis sure is a pretty thing, ain't she, Sheriff?"

"Did you steal a kiss?"

"Nah, warn't time. She heard her sister carryin' on in your office and finally decided to poke her head in."

"You were eavesdropping?"

"I wasn't eavesdroppin'! I was eatin' the candy she done brought me. She sure had *her* ear to the door, though."

Clayton smiled. "Women."

"Maybe now that yer gettin' hitched, Charlotte will take them claws of hers and sink 'em into some other poor fella."

Clayton looked down at Billy, who was easily several inches shorter. "I thought you said you weren't eavesdropping?"

"I warn't! But I couldn't help hearin' most of it, the way Miss Charlotte was screechin' at the top of her lungs."

Clayton laughed at that. "Well, Billy, I hope you're right, and she's done with any plans she may have to marry me. It never would have worked out."

"Maybe. Only the Almighty knows."

They didn't see Charlotte Davis, after turning a corner and heading down another street, put her nose in the air and smile. Within moments of leaving the sheriff's office, she'd devised a plan for getting exactly what she wanted – and getting rid of what she didn't.

Come quitting time, Clayton couldn't wait to get home. The anticipation he felt was familiar, yet so very different at the same time. When Sarah was alive, he used to love coming in from the orchards at suppertime; he couldn't wait to take Sarah in his arms and see what she'd been up to. But this wasn't quite the same. This anticipation made his heart drop into his stomach and his mind begin to race over things to say to the pretty lady he'd find waiting for him at home with his mother.

Most of all, he couldn't wait to sweep her up his arms and carry her in to supper. Last night, when he'd carried her back to her room, he'd lingered a moment or two with her in his arms and teased her about a spot of jam she had at one corner of her lovely mouth. It was all he could do not to kiss the jam away. But it was still too soon to kiss her, no matter how much he wanted to. His future bride needed time, and he wanted her to feel comfortable with him the first time they kissed.

He was amazed that, once he'd decided to marry her, he had started to notice wonderful little details about her. Like how she had dark flecks of a deeper blue in her eyes. Or how her mouth curved up to one side when something amused her. Or the tiny little dimple on the left side of her mouth. The way she blushed whenever he came into the room. The smell of lilac in her hair when he carried her into the dining parlor last night …

"Are you going to wait for me to at least mount up first?" Spencer called after him as he watched Clayton trot away.

Clayton brought his big black gelding to a stop and turned to face him as Spencer mounted his grey mare. "Thought you were right behind me."

"How could I be? You lit on out of that office like your pants were on fire! What's the hurry?"

Clayton smiled. "I've got something waiting for me at home." He winked, turned his horse, and cantered down the street.

Spencer nodded to Billy, who stood smiling in the doorway of the sheriff's office, and they both laughed. Then Spencer put in his spurs and followed his brother.

"Hey, sweet thing – wake up."

Summer's eyes opened slowly. She smiled when she saw Clayton's face bent over hers, his emerald eyes sparkling with something she hadn't seen before. "I must have dozed off. Is it time for supper already?"

"Sure is. Ma told me you had visitors today." He leaned back in the chair by the desk and waited.

"Oh, yes. *Them.*"

"Well, I don't want you to worry about it. I spoke with Charlotte today – she's got a handle on herself. Even wished us the very best."

Summer pushed herself up with her elbows to better look at him. "Really? Did your mother tell you about what happened when they were here?"

"She doesn't have to – I know Charlotte Davis, and her mother. Don't worry about it a second more, okay?"

She let go her breath and sank back into the mattress. "Okay."

"Now it's time, m'lady." He held out his arms in demonstration.

Summer smiled.

Clayton pulled off the quilt she'd used to cover herself earlier, then easily scooped her up and stood. "Ahhhh," he sighed. "I've been waiting for this all day."

She blushed a bright pink at his flirting and wrapped her arms about his neck.

"Tomorrow I have a surprise for you," he told her with a wink.

"A surprise? What sort of surprise?"

"Thanksgiving is only two days away, so tomorrow you and I are going into town to see about getting you a few things."

"Oh, Clayton, you don't have to do that."

He stopped in the hall and looked at her. "Yes, I do. It's a matter of honor – you're to be my wife, and I'll see you dressed and taken care of properly, you hear?"

Summer's heart sank. Was he embarrassed by her? She knew her two dresses were horrible. Charlotte and Nellie Davis had only stated the obvious during their little visit.

"No argument. Tomorrow, we'll see what we can do. Spencer spoke with Abbey Davis while she was in town today, and she's got a few things you can use until we have some dresses made for you."

"Oh, Clayton … wait. Abbey *Davis?*"

"Don't fret – she's much nicer than her mother or sister." He entered the dining parlor and set her down in her chair at the table.

"It's true," Spencer agreed from the kitchen. "She's like the 'white sheep' of the family."

Clayton heard Summer sniffle. "Miss James, are you all right?"

She looked at him and fought the tears welling up. "I am. It's just that … no one has ever done this sort of thing for me before."

He straightened, looked down at her, and smiled. "Well, it's about time someone did, then. And I'm glad to be the one who's doing it."

She swallowed, unable to keep a tear from falling. "So am I."

Clayton sat next to her as his mother and Spencer brought in dinner. Once they were seated he said the blessing, winked at her, and reached for the tureen of stew.

Summer sighed as another tear dropped. She wanted to pinch herself, to make sure she was awake and not dreaming. Her current circumstances seemed too good to be true. So much had happened to her since the day she sat outside Mrs. Ridgley's office not a month ago.

Thank you, Lord, and thank you, Mrs. Ridgley. Summer thought to herself as two realizations suddenly hit her. First, for the first time in a very long time, she was happy. And second? She suspected that the wonderful warm feeling in the center of her very being was more than a simple reaction whenever she saw the handsome Clayton Riley.

In fact, Summer began to suspect she was falling in love.

TEN

The next morning Clayton prepared the wagon for a trip into town. Summer was once again riding in the back on blanket-covered hay, warmly wrapped in quilts while Clayton and his mother sat up front. She tucked the quilts about her tightly as cold blasts of wind swept across the landscape. Growing up in New Orleans had not prepared her for the Northwest in autumn.

But other than the temperature, it was a beautiful day. The sun was bright overhead, without a cloud in the sky, and the air was clean and dry. Apple orchards stood on either side of the road, before giving way to pumpkin fields. She could see a few stray orange gourds still in their rows as they drove by.

Summer sighed and wished it would snow again – but just not at the moment. It wouldn't do to be sitting in the back of a wagon for several miles while it snowed. At least she didn't think so. On the other hand, if she was snuggled against Clayton up front on the wagon seat, it might prove to be quite nice ...

Once they reached town, Clayton parked the

wagon in front of Quinn's Mercantile, set the brake and helped his mother down. Spencer came out and waved. He'd left home right after breakfast for the sheriff's office, so he must have been waiting for them in town.

Spencer hopped up into the back of the wagon. "Good morning! How's my future sister-in-law?" He bent down and scooped her up before she could reply, then deftly handed her down to Clayton's waiting arms.

"Fine," she said as Clayton looked into her eyes and smiled.

Spencer laughed. "Yes, I can see that." He jumped down from the wagon, ran up the steps and back into the mercantile.

Clayton continued to smile and look into her eyes. People stopped and stared at them, and Summer began to feel self-conscious. After all, he was holding her in his arms in public, where everyone could see! Did any of the folks staring at them know of her injury?

"Well, well, there you are!" Mrs. Quinn stood in the doorway of the mercantile. She was a tall, thin, grey-haired woman with a wide grin on her face. "Don't just stand there, Clayton – bring her inside where it's warm! I've got some right pretty things to show you, Miss James!"

Summer smiled at her as Clayton carried her up some stairs, across the boardwalk and into the mercantile. Warmth quickly wrapped around her as he carried her toward the pot-bellied stove near the counter and gently set her in a chair. He took the quilts from her and handed them to Spencer, who folded them up and slid them underneath the chair.

"Oh, you have new ribbons!" Mrs. Riley exclaimed from across the mercantile. "Summer, I must get some of these for you!"

"Oh no, Mrs. Riley ..."

"Stop!" Clayton barked. "There will be no '*oh no Clayton oh no Mrs. Riley*,'" he mimicked. "You are going to sit there and let us take care of you."

Her eyes grew wide. Could this be real? Her breathing became short and her chest tightened. She almost felt as though she would faint! To see someone *want* to take care of her was almost beyond her understanding. Sure, she'd imagined it millions of times, ever since she was a small child. If not dreaming of a set of parents doing it, she'd pictured a family of sorts, or friends, and finally she began dreaming of the day a husband would do this sort of thing.

But now that it was real, she felt queasy and nervous. Would it all simply disappear? When would she find herself fighting for scraps in the streets? But no, she was past that, out of danger. Clayton said he would marry her. And besides, he'd sent for her, hadn't he? She was here, not in New Orleans! There was no Mr. Slade lurking in the dark shadows of an alley waiting to grab and enslave her the first chance he got. She was safe, safe, safe!

But the fear in her heart was old and would not be silenced overnight. She was going to have to work hard to keep it at bay, to silence its relentless screaming that said this was all a mistake, he really didn't want her, it was only a matter of time before he sent her back …

"Do you like the pink or the green better, dear?"

Summer shook herself and forced her eyes to meet Mrs. Riley's. She swallowed hard. "Oh … the pink. I like the pink."

"So do I. It will look lovely with your hair," Mrs. Riley happily agreed. She set the ribbons on the nearby counter, then went to speak with Mrs. Quinn, who was pulling bolts of cloth from a shelf.

Clayton took a chair and pulled it up alongside her. "Now, I want you to tell Ma what fabrics you fancy for a few dresses. You'll need a pair of shoes too, and a coat. Just let Ma know what you like, and she or Mrs. Quinn will fetch it to you to look at. Are you warm enough?"

Summer stared at him, dumbfounded. "I … I …" She swallowed hard. Her head began to spin again, and her heart felt as though it would leap from her chest. She felt herself precariously begin to lean to one side.

"Whoa there, honey!" Clayton exclaimed as he pulled her upright. "What's the matter?"

She took a few deep breaths. What *was* the matter? Good grief! She had an overwhelming urge to go back to the farm and hide in her little room! And all because Clayton was showing her kindness and wanting to take care of her? *Lord, help me! Help me to receive these wonderful gifts and the blessings You're providing! Help me not to mess this up!*

"Do you want me to take you home?" Clayton whispered in her ear.

The fear in her heart leapt to life at the question. *Yes!!!* But she closed her eyes against it. If she gave in and let fear win out, it would only happen again – she had to get a handle on it!

She slowly shook her head. "I'll be all right. Just give me a moment."

Clayton ran a hand over her back a few times. "You take all the time you need, honey. I'm not going anywhere until I know you're all right."

"Is something wrong?" His mother asked as she walked up with a bolt of blue calico in her hands.

"Miss James felt a touch dizzy, I think, but she's fine now," he answered as he put a finger under her chin and turned her face toward his. "Isn't that right?"

Summer nodded, the dizziness gone. She took a deep breath and smiled. "I'm fine now, really."

He eyed her a moment longer before he finally looked satisfied. He turned to his mother. "I need to check on some things, see if there's been any word concerning those outlaws. You'll look after her, won't you, Ma?"

"Of course, dear! Mrs. Quinn and I will be a while yet. Take your time!"

Clayton took one of Summer's hands in his own and stood. "You sure you'll be okay?"

Summer smiled at the concern in his eyes and voice. Her body warmed from the top of her head to the tip of her toes. Could it be he felt something for her? She brightened at the thought, and her smile widened. "Yes, thank you. It's just … it's just that this is all so new for me." She blushed at the admission.

Clayton knelt before her and engulfed her hand in both of his. "Ah, honey, I think I understand. But you have nothing to worry about, not anymore. You're here now, and that's what counts."

She swallowed and tried to sit still as the fear in her heart banged against the door she'd so recently closed on it. She nodded, unable to speak.

He slowly stood. "I'll be back for you. Have fun now." He then turned to Mrs. Quinn. "Get her whatever she wants." He tipped his hat and left.

Mrs. Quinn let go a gasp of delight and clapped her hands in front of her. "Well, I must say, Miss James, but you're a lucky girl this day!"

Summer's breathing escaped in short pants. She fought a rising lump in her throat, one born of the fear that the whole scene would disappear in a puff of smoke, and she'd find herself cold and alone on some New Orleans street running from the likes of Mr. Slade.

"What's the matter? Can't decide on what you fancy most?" Mrs. Quinn asked.

Mrs. Riley took the chair Clayton had so recently occupied. "Betsy, would you bring me that brown calico? I want to show it to Summer."

"Certainly," Mrs. Quinn replied. She turned to do as asked.

Mrs. Riley watched her go, then said, "Now don't you worry about a thing, dear. We have plenty of money to get what we need. In fact, why don't we get some yarn and needles so you can start some knitting for Christmas? It would be the perfect distraction while your foot heals."

"Mrs. Riley," Summer began on a sigh. "It's all ... so much."

"I'm sure it is, dear! Why, I can't imagine what it would be like to travel out here alone to marry a man you've never met, and on top of it let him leave you in the mercantile and tell you to get whatever you want! Though if it were me, I'd especially like that part! But seriously, dear, Clayton is a good man and a good provider. He wants you to have these things, and you need to have them! None of this is frivolous, so don't you be feeling guilty about it."

"None of it?"

"For heaven's sake, no!"

Mrs. Quinn approached with the bolt of brown calico. "Land sakes, child! You're gonna marry the man – let him take care of you!"

Summer took a deep breath. She could do this. "All right, then," she said as she looked first at Mrs. Riley, then at Mrs. Quinn. "Let's shop."

Clayton left the mercantile and marched straight to Doc Brown's. He banged on the door and waited impatiently for someone to answer.

Milly swung open the door with a look of concern, which quickly changed to annoyance when she saw he was alone. "What's all the banging about? Where's the patient?"

"At the mercantile."

"What do you mean, at the mercantile? What's going on?"

"I left Miss James at the mercantile with Ma. She needed some things. But that's not why I'm here. She nearly fainted."

"What?" Milly cried. "Come in, Clayton, and tell me what happened."

Clayton entered the house and followed Milly into the parlor. "She seemed fine, but then she nearly fainted after I set her down in a chair and started to tell her to get what she needed."

"Has she been eating okay?"

"Yes. Sleeping all right too, as far as I know."

"Did something happen to upset her?"

Clayton drew in a deep breath. "Nellie and Charlotte Davis came out to the house yesterday, but that's about it."

Milly frowned. "That would be enough. Those two harpies were buzzing around town yesterday like a pair of hornets. Mark my words; they're up to something. I trust that Nellie Davis about as far as I can toss her!"

"I don't know what it could be. Charlotte's okay with me marrying Miss James – wished me luck and everything."

"Clayton Riley, tell me you're not that stupid."

Clayton looked down at Milly, his eyes

suddenly wide.

"Yeah, you'd better be worried!" she spat. "You're far too trusting. It's amazing that Charlotte hasn't found a way to force you to marry her by now!"

"I don't love her," was Clayton's simple reply.

"Well then, what's the difference between Charlotte Davis and Miss James? Do you love *her*?"

Clayton stiffened. "I ... I ..."

"You'd better make sure your heart's in the right place before you up and marry that girl. True, you *should* marry her, especially after she came all the way out here. Besides, you're a lonely old cuss, and will only get lonelier, and more cussed, if you don't. But court her until you at least start having *some* feelings, or she ain't gonna be no better than if you married Charlotte!"

Clayton let his breath out slowly. Milly had a point – what was the difference? Only that Charlotte would drive him crazy in a matter of months. But at least he knew Charlotte; he didn't really know Miss James.

"Clayton, I've doctored you your entire life. Sarah was my daughter and a good woman, and it's a shame she died so young. Take this girl, fall in love, marry her and start fresh. Heck, let Spencer be sheriff and go back to farming! I bet it would do you good!"

Clayton looked down at her, brow furrowed.

"All I'm really saying is ... well ... let your heart out of that box you put it in the day Sarah died. Don't be afraid to let someone else have it. My guess is, you figure if you marry her right away, you won't have time to feel anything, and love will grow in time. But son, I know you. That's an excuse. Go ahead and court her a little. Get to know her. Give love a head start, before you get hitched. Don't give your heart a chance to bury itself deeper in the ground to hide."

Clayton's jaw clenched. "Milly …"

"Don't you 'Milly' me – I'm as much a ma to you as the one you got at home. Speaking of which, I'm sure Leona loves her already!"

Clayton closed his eyes a moment. His mother *did* love Miss James – made her feel at home, doted on her, took care of her during the day, talked about her to he and Spencer every waking moment. Summer James had brought life back into his mother, and for that he was grateful.

Besides, he realized at that moment, he *was* starting to have feelings for Summer. At first he'd thought it was simple attraction. She was a beautiful woman, very beautiful, but there were a lot of beautiful women out there. Even Charlotte Davis was quite fetching until she opened her mouth. But this was something more – he'd begun to find it difficult to take his eyes off of Summer, to not think about her during the day.

"I hate it when you're right, Milly."

"I know you do. Now stop your worrying. I'll have Doc drop by your place later this afternoon and check on her. Will that settle you down?"

Clayton nodded. "Thanks, Milly. I knew I could count on you."

"Count on me for what?"

"For doctoring me – in this case, my heart. You're right. I need to let it loose instead of keeping it corralled. I'll court Miss James properly, then marry her."

"Good! Now, go fall in love. Doctor's orders."

"Yes, ma'am." Clayton smiled, winked, then got up and left the house.

By the time Mrs. Riley and Mrs. Quinn were done with her, Summer had in her possession four different kinds of calico fabric, a new pair of shoes, a coat, several different skeins of yarn, two sets of knitting needles, a new hairbrush and half a dozen colored ribbons. It was more than she'd ever owned in her lifetime, and Clayton Riley had given it all to her. Mrs. Riley was just paying the bill when the bell over the door rang.

Summer's heart sank as Nellie Davis strolled into the store like a queen, Charlotte close on her heels. "Why, there you are, Leona! I thought I saw your wagon in town," Nellie crooned.

"How can you possibly miss it? It's parked right outside," Mrs. Riley pointed out dryly.

Nellie ignored her and glided up to the counter, eyeing the purchases Mrs. Quinn was wrapping up in brown paper. "My, my, whatever do we have here? Is this all yours, Leona? Are we Christmas shopping?"

"I'm shopping for Summer. Clayton wanted her to have some new dresses and a few other things."

"Summer?" Nellie asked feigning ignorance. "Oh, you mean that horrid creature staying at your house? Don't tell me you're keeping her?"

Charlotte placed herself right next to Summer. "Mother, really now! She's right here!"

Summer immediately became suspicious at the girl speaking in her defense.

Nellie turned. "Oh, so she is. Well, I suppose if you're going to be that stubborn about it, all we can do is help you out."

"I don't need any help from you, Nellie Davis." Mrs. Riley said. "Mrs. Jorgensen can whip up anything we need."

"Oh, but I'm afraid you'll be out of luck. I just spoke with Mrs. Jorgensen yesterday and she's busier than a bee this season making things for folks for Christmas. She couldn't possibly take any more work on."

"She doesn't need to," Summer said. "I can sew my own clothes."

Nellie looked her up and down with disapproval. "Yes, we've all seen how well you sew, haven't we?"

"Summer, you don't have to worry about a thing. I'll make whatever you need if Mrs. Jorgensen is too busy," Mrs. Riley told her with a smile.

Summer caught the flash of anger in her eyes as she quickly glanced at Nellie Davis. "I know you will, and I so appreciate it."

"But what about your wedding dress?" Charlotte asked innocently. "Mrs. Jorgensen is too busy, and you can't expect Mrs. Riley to make *everything* for you. That would be taking advantage of her, don't you think?"

"I'm sure we'll both be working on the dresses together," Summer said diplomatically, though her hands were balling into fists in her lap.

"Still, that's a lot of work to do," Nellie began. "I'm afraid you'll have to postpone your wedding until the dress is done. Too bad Mrs. Jorgensen is so dreadfully busy, or she could have finished it for you in no time."

Summer and Mrs. Riley were both about to comment when Clayton strolled through the mercantile's door.

"Why, Clayton!" Charlotte exclaimed and all but ran to him. She quickly wrapped an arm around one of his and snuggled against him. "It's so nice to see you! We were just talking about wedding dresses!"

Clayton looked down at her as if he was being hugged by a garter snake – harmless, but still annoying. "Were you, now?"

Summer watched, and tried to fight a sudden wave of jealousy. Despair soon followed and pierced her heart, freeing the familiar fear. *No, no, no!* she told herself. *Don't let it take over!*

"It's too bad you can't get married right away," Nellie began. "What with the time it takes to make a dress and all. A lot can happen between now and then."

"I'm not worried about it," Clayton said and smiled.

Charlotte tightened her grip on his arm before she stood on tip-toe to whisper in his ear. "You mean you're not in any hurry to get married?" Naturally, she whispered loud enough for everyone in the room to hear.

Summer closed her eyes for a moment and took a deep breath.

"No," he said calmly. "There's no rush."

Summer's heart sank. Charlotte stood straighter and then, to everyone's surprise, kissed him on the cheek. "I thought as much." She released him and sent Summer a triumphant smile before she turned to her mother.

"Well, I guess you won't be doing as much sewing as you thought, Leona," Nellie said without looking at her and started for the door.

Clayton ignored both the Davis women as he moved next to the chair Summer sat in. She felt the heat of his body, took in the sheer size of him, the broadness of his chest and shoulders as he towered over her. "Is everything settled here?" he asked Mrs. Quinn.

"Yes, Clayton. We're all done," Mrs. Quinn said as she glared at the Davis women.

"Good," he said and quickly scooped Summer up into his arms. "C'mon, honey, let's go have us some lunch over at Hank's restaurant. Old Hank makes a mean bean soup!"

Nellie and Charlotte's mouths dropped open at the same time. "You mean you're going to carry her all the way down to Hank's?" Charlotte asked in shock.

"How else would I get her there?" Clayton asked. "She can't walk yet."

"You can't carry her down the street in public!" Nellie gasped.

"Why not? The whole town knows she's injured. Makes perfect sense to me."

"Clayton Riley! You *cannot* carry her!" Charlotte whined.

Clayton looked at Summer. Her fear had immediately disappeared the moment he'd lifted her into his arms. His strength was incredible, the warmth of his body intoxicating. He smiled down at her, then returned his gaze to Charlotte. "As a matter of fact, I can. And I can't think of anything I'd like to do more than carry this pretty little lady to lunch."

"But, but ... everyone will see!" Nellie scolded.

Clayton smirked at her. "Yes, Mrs. Davis. I know." He winked at the woman, turned on his heel and left the mercantile with his future bride in his arms.

It was all Summer could do not to let the water works start. He'd just championed her in front of Mrs. Davis *and* her daughter – slapped them with the fact that he cared about her. She took in a shaky breath as the cold and the bright sunshine hit her.

"Close your eyes, honey, and enjoy the ride," he whispered in her ear.

Summer did, at least for a moment, as she realized she could fall deeply and madly in love with Clayton Riley. And, in fact, already was.

ELEVEN

Thanksgiving dawned bright and cold. Summer awoke early to the clatter of pots and pans coming from the kitchen as Mrs. Riley began her day. She wanted to be in the kitchen to help her, and struggled trying to get out of bed and dressed. She could at least hobble around at this point, but still had to be very careful. The doctor from town had paid a surprise visit to her two days before and checked her foot. In fact, he'd kept checking her for fever as well, but she knew she didn't have one … at least, not the kind the doctor suspected. No, her flushed face, rapid heart and goose-pimpled flesh was not from any sort of cold or flu, but from Clayton Riley.

The minute Summer remembered how Clayton had carried her through town to take her to lunch, her heart began to race, she blushed something awful and delightful chills went up her spine. She couldn't stop thinking about it after he drove them home, got her settled, then rode back into town to finish out his day at the sheriff's office.

It wasn't long after that the doctor had showed up - but the doctor hadn't seen what Clayton did, had no idea how he'd championed her in front of the Davis women. His actions made her feel much more secure – and the look on Charlotte Davis's face was priceless!

By the time Mrs. Riley had joined them at Hank's restaurant, Summer felt as if she was a beautiful damsel in distress, just rescued by a handsome prince. A silly dream she'd had so often as a child had just been fulfilled, and nothing could dampen her spirits. It was the best day of her life, and she knew she would treasure it always.

"Oh good, you're up," Clayton said as he poked his head into the room. "Ma could sure use your help in the kitchen. I'd do it, but Spencer and I have to run into town to check on some things. We'll be back in plenty of time for supper."

Summer clutched at her nightdress and looked at him. She noted how he nonchalantly studied her in the early morning light from the window. Heat shot through her like gunfire, and she sucked in a breath. Good heavens, but he was handsome! "Do ... do you have to go?" she asked, suddenly unable to bear the thought of him leaving her at all.

He smiled. "Well, honey, I can think of better ways to spend my time than having a meeting with a tired-out posse, but duty calls." He stepped into the room, and she pulled the nightdress more closely as he bent over her. His voice dropped in pitch. "In fact I can think of a *lot* of things I'd rather be doing." He stroked her cheek with the back of his hand and smiled. "I'll send in Ma to help you dress, then I'll help you into the kitchen."

Summer felt her stomach somersault. Her breathing slowed and she couldn't get any words to come out, as if his touch had rendered her completely speechless. All she could do was look up at him and nod.

He lingered a moment longer, quietly staring down at her. He closed his eyes and turned his face a second before he pulled his hand away, as if it pained him to do it. "I'll be back with Ma. Don't go anywhere now, you hear?"

She smiled. "I won't." He left the room and she sighed. Oh, Lord, how could she stand it? One minute her heart fluttered wildly in her chest, her whole being somehow engulfed by Clayton's presence ... no, his *essence*. Then just as suddenly, the familiar cold fear would come, reminding her that it could all disappear in a puff of smoke.

But not today! She forced her heart to still and let herself enjoy the warmth from his hand against her cheek, the scent of wind and soap and leather that surrounded him, the knowledge that soon she would be his completely ...

If only he would just marry her! Why was he waiting? Yes, her foot ... she knew that made him take pause. He wanted her to be able to stand for their wedding. But her insecurities would not still so easily, and she had to constantly fight to keep her emotions under control. She hoped that today, they too would take a holiday and leave her alone.

Mrs. Riley helped her dress, and soon Clayton had carried her into the kitchen, where he sat her down at the table. Then, much to Summer's surprise, he kissed her on the cheek. "See you later, darling. Ma, don't tire her out." He put on his hat and left through the back door.

"My, my, that son of mine certainly is in a good mood this morning," Mrs. Riley said then gave her a wink.

Summer swallowed and tried to come down from the cloud she was floating on. "Yes, ma'am."

Mrs. Riley laughed as she set a roasting pan down in front of her on the table. The turkey was larger than any Summer had seen at Winslow – it barely fit in the large pan. "Now let's stuff this bird and get things underway. Those boys of mine are gonna be mighty hungry when they get home."

Summer smiled as she took it all in: the warmth of the kitchen, the smell of pies in the oven, the dinner they were preparing for the men and their guests later that day. This was already the *second* most wonderful day in her life!

Clayton frowned at the news the posse brought back. He'd hoped he wouldn't have to worry about the notorious outlaw Red Ned and his gang of cutthroats on this of all days, but he wasn't going to be so fortunate. They'd been spotted not twenty miles from Nowhere, and that didn't set well with him, not one tiny bit.

The men were tired, hurting, hungry and in a generally foul mood after that combination of hard riding, bad news and no results to show for it. He told them all to go home and take today and the next day off. They deserved the rest and time with their families.

"Red Ned," he mumbled to himself after they'd left. "Who comes up with these names?"

"Locals, usually," Spencer commented from behind him. "Or a newspaper reporter with too much imagination." He stared at the wanted poster over Clayton's shoulder. "Ned's spilled enough blood to have earned it, though, that's for sure."

"Yeah. Well, Ned had better not interrupt our dinner tonight, that's all I can say," Clayton grumbled as he reached for his hat. "Are you ready?"

Spencer grabbed his own hat. "As ready as I'll ever be. Let's do our rounds and make sure everything's nice and quiet, then go home and eat. I'm starved already!"

"Sure hope Billy's enjoying his holiday supper. I wonder if Miss Abbey will come down and bring him some pie this evening while he's on duty."

"Ha! Not if her sister Charlotte can help it. Now that you're taken, she's probably looking for some other unsuspecting prey."

"'Unsuspecting prey,' Spence?"

"Yeah, as in any unmarried man within fifty

miles of here," Spencer replied with a laugh.

Clayton eyed him before his face broke into a smile. "Well, little brother, that would include you. Fancy that."

Spencer's laughter abruptly stopped. "Sam blazes, you're right."

"Maybe I oughta send you out with the next posse so Charlotte doesn't have a chance to get a hold of you."

Spencer gulped. "That might not be a bad idea." The two men laughed, put on their hats, and left the sheriff's office to make their rounds.

It was the longest set of rounds Sheriff Clayton Riley could remember. Spencer was in an exceptionally good mood, which made the day go by quicker, but didn't take Clayton's mind off of who was waiting for him at home.

He was beginning to enjoy the idea of getting married. Even more so, he was enjoying the idea of courting Miss Summer James until she couldn't stand it any longer. He wanted to carry her to the altar, not because of her foot or that he had to force her, but because she'd be so enamored with him she'd be weak in the knees and swooning.

He smiled at the thought. Yes sir, he'd court her like no woman had ever been courted before. He'd make sure she felt something for him, and he planned on having fun doing it, too!

He relaxed as they rode from farm to farm, giving folks the warning to keep an eye out for Red Ned and take no chances when it came to strangers. But not even the news they delivered could dampen his mood. He was exceptionally happy and, for the first time in a long time, didn't think about the emptiness of his heart or the void left there after Sarah's death. He realized he'd found something to fill it.

Yes siree, Summer James had no idea what was coming her way!

Thanksgiving came and went. Forget second place, and forget yesterday – *this* was the most wonderful day of Summer's life! The food was incredible, and she'd helped to prepare it. Doc and Milly Brown were delightful company, and she enjoyed Milly's stories of when the Riley brothers were children. Mrs. Riley shared her own tales (much to Clayton and Spencer's horror), and Summer laughed until her sides hurt and she couldn't see for the tears in her eyes.

But the best part of the day came after the pumpkin pie and coffee, when Clayton carried her into the parlor while the others talked around the dining room table. He set her down and sat next to her, his body so close their shoulders were touching. "That was a lovely meal – thank you, honey," he told her, his voice soft and low. "I can't remember when I've eaten so much."

She smiled and blushed at the compliment. The lamplight was dim, and she wondered if he had slipped into the parlor earlier and turned it down. The smell of the rich food hung in the air, mixed with Clayton's own intoxicating scent. She felt tired from the day's labors, what few she'd been able to perform, and wanted nothing more than to rest her head against his shoulder. But she didn't dare, it would be improper. Growing up in the orphanage, Mrs. Teeters had taught her what was what.

But Mrs. Teeters hadn't taught Summer what to do when Clayton put an arm across the back of the settee and leaned toward her. His face was so close she could feel the breath escape his lips as he spoke. "Today was a mighty fine day. And you know what would make it even finer?"

She melted at the sound of his voice, his face so close to hers. She sat and looked straight ahead, afraid to look at him, afraid the closeness would be too much for her to bear. He'd been carrying her around for over a week – one would think she'd be able to face him. But her fear was rising again – what would she see if she turned to him? Would he be looking at her with lust or admiration, indecision or loving intent?

How did he feel about her, really? He hadn't said one thing about their wedding or, more importantly, the date. Dinner had been taken up with talk of the outlaws they'd been searching for and stories of his childhood antics. In fact, not once did *anyone* at the table mention anything pertaining to their upcoming marriage.

Summer's heart sank at the thought, and she fought the fear that squeezed her chest so tightly she wondered that she could breathe at all.

"Is there something the matter, honey?"

Clayton suddenly asked.

She closed her eyes and quickly shook her head.

"Are you sure? You don't look so good."

"I'm sure. I'm sorry, I guess I'm just tired."

Clayton removed his arm from behind her, placed his hands on his legs and sighed. "Well then, maybe you ought to turn in," he said, his voice suddenly flat.

No, no, no! Summer, stop it – stop it now! But the fear had her, and she felt her heart dive straight into disappointment. The same disappointment that gripped her whenever she heard Mrs. Teeters say, *I'm sorry she didn't suit you, but we have other children who might ...*

Nooooo! She screamed in her head as Clayton let go a heavy sigh. *Please, God, make this stop! Why does it always have to come and ruin everything?*

"All right, let's get you to your room," Clayton said as he stood. He turned to her, regret written all over his face as he unceremoniously scooped her up from the settee and turned toward the hall.

No, please, not yet! But it was as if an invisible gag had been placed on her. She couldn't tell him to stop, that she wanted him to hold her, how she was beginning to feel. She began to wonder if she ever would ...

Her stomach knotted up and she felt the first hot sting of tears as he pushed the door to her room open with his foot, went in and set her on the bed. Her entire body went cold, and she felt the familiar bracing of her spine, the tightness in her chest, as he looked down on her, his face an expressionless mask.

"Are you sure you're all right?"

She would *not* start crying! How could she explain herself if she did? What would he think? She quickly nodded without looking at him.

He went to one knee in front of her and took her face in his hands. "You wouldn't be lying to me now, would you?"

Her eyes widened. "No," came out, barely a whisper.

"Well … then you get some sleep, honey. You do look plumb tuckered out." But he didn't let go. Instead he knelt and stared into her eyes as if searching for something. His head cocked to one side as he studied her further, then his eyes went to her mouth and stayed there.

She sucked in a breath. Good Lord, was he going to kiss her? *Why would he do that? Why on earth would he kiss you? Why? Why? Why?* The voice of fear screamed in her head. Always, when the hope of love at long last realized came, it shouted and drove her in the opposite direction.

She stifled a sob as he looked at her, his head slowly coming closer. But he abruptly stopped, turned his head away and sighed. "All right then," he said. When he again looked at her, his face was calm, his expression blank. "Get some sleep." He stood and left the room.

As the door closed behind him, the hot tears of disappointment began to stream down her face, the voice of fear loud and triumphant. *See? See?!? He left you, just like all the others. He doesn't want you! Who would ever want you?*

Summer turned, fell into her pillow and screamed. "Shut up! Go away, just go away!"

Fear finally departed. But it left behind what it always did: a heart broken by a lifetime of rejection and disappointment, a life lived day-to-day with the knowledge that she would always be alone. And one day, she would die the same way – alone and unwanted.

"Why, Lord? Why now, when I've met someone who wants me, I can't let him? Why? Please, please heal me from this!" But she felt no comfort like she sometimes had in the past. Instead, the tears continued in violent waves.

By the time Mrs. Riley came into the room to check on her, it was to find Summer's head on a wet pillow, her tear-stained face red from crying, and her body so exhausted from her recent battle with herself she slept as if dead.

Mrs. Riley looked at her and brushed away her own tears before she knelt down beside the bed and did the one thing she knew would help. She prayed.

TWELVE

The next week passed with eerie repetition for Summer. Clayton and Spencer left before dawn every day, and came home late for supper every night. At the end of the week, they announced they were heading out with the posse for a few days in search of the outlaw called Red Ned.

She'd gone from being the happiest girl in the world for a brief few days to feeling nothing but an odd numbness. It was how she always felt after a couple had rejected her at the orphanage. Why would she feel any different here? Of course, Clayton hadn't told her he didn't want to marry her anymore, but why else would he be spending so much time away from the farm? Often Mrs. Riley helped her to her room and into bed. She hopped from room to room during the day, and on Friday was delighted when Doc Brown brought her a pair of crutches. Now at least she could go outside and help Mrs. Riley with more of the work.

She fed the chickens and did other simple tasks around the barnyard, and even though it was growing colder by the day, she enjoyed the time spent out-of-doors. It gave her a chance to think and decide what to do. Several times she sat on the porch swing and let the cold air embrace her – once so much that she barely managed to get out of the swing with Mrs. Riley's help. She received quite the scolding for letting herself get so cold, and decided to be more careful from then on. She didn't want Mrs. Riley to worry.

And the woman *was* worried – Summer could see it in her eyes whenever she looked at her. Perhaps it was because she suspected her son was pulling away from his bride-to-be as well, that it was only a matter of time before he announced he'd changed his mind and would send her back.

Summer thought on the possibility all week. Why else would he be staying away? He'd hardly spoken three words to her since Thanksgiving! And now he was gone completely, for who knew how long! How many days *would* it be before they returned?

As it turned out, Clayton and Spencer were gone off and on for nearly three weeks before they finally returned from their search, unsuccessful and worn out. They got home and without a word crawled up the stairs to their rooms. And they weren't heard from again until early afternoon the next day, when Summer happened to be in the kitchen peeling apples for a pie.

She stopped breathing when Clayton entered the kitchen and headed for the stove. She'd kept the pot of coffee warm for when they did get up, but worried it would be too old and stale by now. She watched as he poured himself a cup, ran a hand through his sleep-tousled hair, and came to the kitchen table. He noted the crutches that she'd propped against a chair but said nothing, just stood and stared at them.

Then he looked at her, and she felt herself go cold. His eyes were expressionless, and he still said nothing. She felt she might as well pack her things up and head to town right now.

"Clayton, sit down and I'll make you something to eat," Mrs. Riley said as she came into the kitchen. "Is Spencer up yet? My, but you look a fright!"

He slowly looked at her and shook his head. He took another sip of coffee before he again turned to Summer, his body still as a statue, and stared.

It was all she could do to sit under that gaze. What was he thinking? Why didn't he just say it? *I've changed my mind, I've thought about it while I was out searching with the posse, and I've decided we just won't suit.* Or, alternatively, *I realized out on the trail how much I missed you – let's go to the preacher right now!* Or anything in between. Something!

Finally Summer could stand the silence no longer. "I think I'll go finish the mending now," she choked out as she reached for the crutches.

Clayton numbly looked at her as his eyes narrowed to slits.

"What?" she suddenly demanded. "What is it you want to say to me?" She was angry now –

angry at him for toying with her, angry that he wouldn't say what he needed to say, whatever it was, and get it over with!

But all he did was stare, his face like stone as he slugged down what coffee was left in the cup. He looked to his mother and said, "I have to go to town," then turned and left without another word.

Summer couldn't help what she did next. She choked back the tears threatening to erupt and went to her room. She would leave, and right now. Enough of this torture! She'd pack up her things and hop to town if she had to!

Mrs. Riley followed her to her room. "Now, don't think he's upset with you, dear. Something's eating him, that's for certain, but I'm sure it has nothing to do with you."

"Nothing?" Summer blurted. "How can you say that? Did you *see* the way he was looking at me? He's going to send me away, Mrs. Riley. I just know it!" She turned from her then, ashamed of her outburst, ashamed to speak so harshly to a woman who had shown her nothing but kindness. Oh, how she wished she could stay! But how could she, knowing Clayton was done with her?

"Don't say that!" Mrs. Riley ordered. "Neither one of us knows what's wrong with that boy, but rest assured I'm going to find out!" She spun on her heel and stomped out of the room.

Summer listened as the back door of the kitchen opened and slammed shut. Fine, let Mrs. Riley hear it before she did. Let Clayton tell his mother what he was going to do. Summer would make sure she wouldn't be around long enough for him to tell her! She'd have Spencer drive her into town, then ask Doc and Milly if she could stay with them a few days until she could make other arrangements.

Of course, Clayton would be sure to make arrangements – arrangements for her to leave, that is. And she was certain she wouldn't have to wait long. But she couldn't stand the thought of hearing him say it, that he was sending her back like an ill-fitting sweater. If only she could escape without seeing him, without having to talk to him. Perhaps then her heart wouldn't completely shatter and break.

Break. Why does a heart break? Why should it feel anything at all about a man she didn't really know, and likely never would? Unless …

"Oh Summer …" she said to herself as realization hit. "Why'd you have to go and fall in love?"

She sat on the bed and closed her eyes. When did it happen? She'd been fearful for the last three weeks, ever since Thanksgiving night! Sure, she'd tried to stay occupied by helping Mrs. Riley sew the dresses she was making for her. She was wearing the brown calico now – which Clayton hadn't even noticed!

She looked about her room at the few things she had. She stood, hopped to the trunk at the end of the bed and picked up the blue calico dress they'd finished just last night. It was beautiful, and she felt guilty about taking it with her. Perhaps she should leave with only what she'd originally brought …

She struggled to kneel and pull her satchel out from under the bed. She pushed herself up, threw it down on the mattress and opened it.

"Going somewhere?" a familiar voice cooed from behind her.

Summer inwardly groaned as she turned around.

Charlotte Davis glided into the room and glanced about. "My, my! Packing already? Oh, I'm so sorry!"

Summer stood straight and squared her shoulders. She would not let this nose-in-the-air plantation belle see how upset she was! "It never would have worked out anyway. It's for the best." She'd let her anger take control, arm her for what was happening. Nothing like adding insult to injury – now she had to deal with this!

"Where is everyone? I drove up and knocked on the door, but no one answered," Charlotte asked with what might've convinced someone else was genuine concern.

Summer didn't buy it for a moment "Clayton … went to town. Mrs. Riley must still be in the barn. She'll be back in a moment, I'm sure." Her sentences were clipped as her fury rose.

"Oh, that explains it. And Spencer? Is he all right?"

"He's asleep. Now if you'll excuse me, I'm very busy."

"I can see that. Leaving, are you?"

"Why else would one pack?" Summer said through clenched teeth. It was all she could do to keep her control.

"I'm so sorry, really I am. It's such a terrible thing. Tell you what – I'll drive you into town so you don't have to disturb Spencer."

Summer froze. Here was her chance, her chance to run from the pain, run from the heartbreak that was sure to come if she heard it from Clayton himself. From anyone else, she'd jump at the opportunity. But from Charlotte Davis ... "What are you doing here, anyway?"

"I came to see if Clayton and Spencer were okay. Billy Blake came over to the house to see Abbey after the posse got back to town. They all had a rough time of it out there. More men were wounded …"

Summer's face fell. "What? How many?"

"At least five. That nasty outlaw Red Ned has been giving our men a heap of trouble these last couple of months."

Summer closed her eyes a moment. How could she be so selfish? Here she was worried about what Clayton was going to do with her, and she hadn't given one thought to what might have happened to him while searching for a bloodthirsty outlaw. "What am I doing?" she whispered to herself.

"Packing," Charlotte answered hopefully.

Summer again looked at her. "Take me to town. I … I need to go to town."

"Yes, I'd be happy to. Let's hurry then."

Summer grabbed the crutches and went to get her coat near the front door.

"Aren't you forgetting something?" Charlotte called after her.

"No, let's just go! I have to talk to Clayton!" Summer called back as she quickly put the coat on.

"All right, I'm coming," Charlotte said as she quickly glanced about the room again. She then stuffed the blue dress into the satchel, grabbed whatever other personal items she could find, threw them in, and then promptly tossed the satchel into the trunk at the end of the bed. She smoothed back her hair, then sashayed down the hall to the front door. "Let's hurry so you can catch him before he heads out anywhere."

Summer stopped and looked at her. "Thank you."

Charlotte smiled broadly. "Oh, don't mention it. I can see you're a woman in love."

Summer too smiled. "Yes – yes, I am." She turned and headed out the door.

Charlotte's smile quickly faded as she watched Summer hobble down the steps and head to the buggy. "But if I play my cards right," she muttered to herself, "Clayton will never find out."

Mrs. Riley pushed herself up from the barn floor. She hadn't been able to talk to Clayton, probably because Clayton hadn't talked at all. He said nothing to her as she came into the barn while he quickly saddled his horse, nothing as she implored him to tell her what was wrong with him, and when he did finally speak, it was only to say that he was riding over to the Johnsons' farm adjacent to their own to see Mr. Johnson before he went to town. He rode out of the barn, took off through the orchards to the neighboring farm and never looked back.

She'd sunk to her knees then and heaved a sob. What was wrong with her boy? She'd never seen him so bleak. What happened to him while he was out there this time? He'd gone out with other posses, but never had he come back so distraught, so full of despair!

She prayed then, prayed and wept for Clayton, for both her sons. And while she cried out to God, she never heard the buggy when it pulled up, nor when it left. So when she finally dried her tears and made her way back to the house, it was with shock and worry that she discovered Summer had disappeared.

Charlotte kept the horse at a good trot all the way to town, keeping up a string of small talk all the way. Summer noted how well the woman could handle the horse and buggy as they drove. She was somewhat jealous, but then it wasn't something she couldn't learn to do herself at some point. Maybe Clayton would teach her.

She sniffed back a tear at the thought. Clayton – she *had* to talk to him! She'd tell him just how she felt, tell him now while her usual fear was suffocated by anger! The fear, she knew, wouldn't let her speak – it bound and gagged her as sure as any ropes or strips of cloth could. But she was determined not to let it this time!

The moment Charlotte told her how bad it had been for Clayton, Spencer, and the rest of the posse on their last search, her heart had broken – not because of rejection or any thoughts of Clayton sending her away, but because of what Clayton must have been through. It had to have been horrible. She knew how he felt about his men, about any man that rode with him. Many of them had families of their own; Mrs. Riley had told her so. Who knew what horrors they had seen or suffered in the search for the outlaw gang that was terrorizing the farms and surrounding towns?

Suddenly, what she felt didn't matter. She needed to make sure Clayton was all right. It was as if he'd been in shock when he'd looked at her earlier – as if he'd seen something so terrible, he couldn't speak of it. She knew what that was like. She had experienced it herself whenever a fellow orphan died – which was often, as many of them had arrived at Winslow in sorry shape. And she had seen it in the eyes of the men who'd returned from the war, the lights in their eyes extinguished by the horrors of battle and the lost cause of the Confederacy that had chewed them up and spit them out without so much as a by-your-leave.

She sniffled a few more times as Charlotte pulled the buggy up in front of the sheriff's office. "I can help you down, or I can go in first and see if he's here," she sweetly offered.

"I'll get down." Summer said, and immediately began to maneuver herself to do just that. She didn't care if she hurt her foot, she had to talk to Clayton!

Charlotte helped her, and Summer was beginning to believe the woman really had let bygones be bygones and was trying to help. She clung to the thought as they went up the steps, crossed the boardwalk and stepped to the door of the sheriff's office.

Charlotte tried the knob but it wouldn't open. "Oh dear," she said.

"It's locked?" Summer asked in shock.

"Try it yourself."

Summer tried the door. It was, indeed. "Where could they be?"

"They might have ridden out already to start another search. I'm sorry we didn't catch Clayton before they left."

Summer's heart sank. "So am I. I really needed to speak with him before …"

"Before you leave? Oh, Miss James, I am sorry!"

Summer glanced at Charlotte, who stood there looking empathetic. But how real was it? She still didn't trust her fully. "I suppose I should have you take me back to the farm. I'm sorry you drove me all the way into town like this, but it was ever so kind of you."

"Oh, now, don't you worry about it. I'll tell you what, why don't you come sit a spell at my house? I'm sure Abbey would love to see you. She's been dying to meet you, and we'd love the company this afternoon. Mother and Daddy have gone over to our uncle's house to look at a horse. They won't be back until suppertime."

Summer noted how Charlotte mentioned Mrs. Davis wouldn't be there. In other words, she would be safe from the woman's comments about how unfitting she was to be Clayton's wife. Even if it appeared Charlotte had turned over a new leaf, she doubted her mother had. "I suppose it would be all right. You are closer to town than the farm …"

"Oh, and Mrs. Riley won't mind. After all, she didn't say anything when we left and I'm sure she saw us."

Summer hadn't thought of that. In fact, she wondered why Clayton's mother hadn't come out of the barn at all.

"Now let's get you out of the cold and have some nice hot tea with Abbey," Charlotte said as she took her arm and pulled her away from the door. Summer hopped down the steps of the boardwalk and back to the buggy. Charlotte helped her up, then turned back to the sheriff's office. "I'll leave Clayton a note and let him know where you are," she suggested.

Now why hadn't she thought of that? Summer silently chided herself for having overlooked something so simple. "Good idea."

"I have a piece of paper and a pencil in my reticule – I can slip the message under the door." Charlotte went to the door, reticule in hand, and pulled out what she needed. She wrote the note, slipped it under the door just as she said she would, then came back to the buggy and climbed in. "There, all done! Now let's go to my house and have some tea and biscuits."

Summer felt a pang of guilt. The woman was being so incredibly helpful. Maybe she had misjudged her, and her previous rudeness was a by-product of following her mother's example. Maybe she really was trying to help. She sighed wearily. "Tea sounds wonderful. Thank you, Charlotte. For everything."

Charlotte gave her a sweet smile. "Don't mention it."

THIRTEEN

It was mid-afternoon by the time Clayton finally made it to town. He rode straight to the sheriff's office, dismounted, and trudged up the steps to the boardwalk. The town of Nowhere was quiet. Most folks were probably done with whatever errands brought them there and had headed home to supper. He wished he was. He missed Summer, and he was going to have to explain his earlier behavior to her when he got home. But first, he had work to do.

He went to enter the office, but the door was locked. Billy must still be making rounds, letting folks know of the danger nearby. It also meant Spencer was still back at the farm. Poor Spence – he'd taken a nasty fall and got quite a bump on the head. Ma was going to go crazy with worry when she saw it. He had meant to stop by Doc Brown's and have him go out to take a look at it. If he was lucky, Doc had already gone to check on not only his brother, but Summer as well. Unfortunately, he hadn't had the chance to yet; he made a mental note to stop by Doc's house before going home.

Clayton unlocked the door and went inside. The office was full of shadows at this time of day and he had to light a lamp just to be able to write out his reports and letters. He wearily sat at the desk and worked for the next several hours. By the time he was done, it was pitch-dark outside, and an effort to get up out of his chair.

Just as he managed to stand up, Billy entered. "You look like somethin' a cat drug in!"

"I feel like it too," was all Clayton managed. He leaned against the desk, folded his arms over his chest, and heaved a weary sigh. "I don't know when I've been as tired."

"Not too tired, I hope! Not with that pretty little thing you got waitin' at home for ya!"

Clayton smiled as he let his head drop to his chest, his eyes closed. They were dry, like someone had thrown sand in them. When he opened them he noticed something on the floor. He squinted and cocked his head to one side as if that would help him see any better.

"What is it?" Billy asked.

"Move your foot," he instructed.

Billy did and looked down. "Hey, what's that?"

"A note. Hand it to me, will you?"

Billy snatched up the note and handed it to him.

Clayton's name was written in neat script on the folded paper. He opened the note and began to read. His eyes immediately widened at the first two words. He looked up from the note in his hand, his mouth wide open in shock. He blinked a few times and looked at it again:

I'm leaving.

Sincerely,
Miss James

Clayton's heart stopped. He knew he should have explained himself before he left the house, but he was still in shock, still too focused on his family and his farm. He'd lit out of the barn and went straight to the Johnsons' to let Mr. Johnson know he was ready to get back to farming and that he would let him go from the lease or, if Mr. Johnson wanted, he could finish out the year.

He'd then ridden into town to write the necessary letters to let his superiors know he was retiring from the office of sheriff and going back to farming. He was done with chasing outlaws, with seeing bodies strung out like a trail of blood across the wilderness. Red Ned had terrorized too many folks of late, and he realized that while he was out protecting Nowhere and its townsfolk from such outlaws, he himself was neglecting to protect his own. How could he continue to put his life in danger day in and day out with a wife depending on him? No, he would make sure he could be with her, be at home to care for his family. It was time to make a change, to go back where he belonged, to finally let go of the past. To let go of Sarah's death.

But now this … Clayton folded the note and

shoved it into his shirt pocket. "Was there a stage coming into town today?"

"I reckon so."

Clayton stopped breathing. "What time did it leave?"

Billy scratched his head. "The usual time, I'd think – two o'clock or thereabouts."

"Good God!" Clayton grabbed his hat and shoved it onto his head. "It's after eight! I'll never catch her!"

"You okay, boss?"

Clayton grabbed Billy by the shoulders and shook him. "Did you see Miss James in town today?"

"No, I done just got back to town myself."

"Did you go to my farm?"

"Well … no. Why would I when I knew you were already out there? 'Sides, Spencer's home, ain't he?"

"He's wounded. Oh God, I need to … to …" Clayton's face took on a sudden look of determination as he headed for the door. "Tell Doc Brown to head out to my place, and have him check on Spencer."

"Where you goin'?"

"To see if Miss James is on that stage!"

"What?"

"She's gone, Billy! She left! There's no good reason for it, no good reason at all!" With that he stormed out of the sheriff's office.

Billy watched as Clayton mounted his big black, kicked him into a gallop, and headed down the street. "Woooeee," he mumbled to himself as he watched his boss ride out of sight.

"Now that there's a man in love." He chuckled, closed the door to the sheriff's office and, whistling, headed for his horse.

"How did you like your chicken, Miss James?" Mr. Davis asked.

Summer stared at her plate. The dinner was delicious, but the company wasn't. Mr. and Mrs. Davis had returned home over two hours ago, and Summer was still trying to fathom how she went from putting on her coat at the sight of them to sitting down to fried chicken and mashed potatoes. She looked at him and forced a smile. "Quite fine."

"Glad to hear it!" Mr. Davis said as he slapped a hand on the table. "If you think that was good, wait until you try the cake Abbey made! She's quite the cook, our little Abbey!"

Summer nodded. Mr. Davis was a balding, portly fellow with fat cheeks and twinkling blue eyes. How could this jovial, pleasant man be married to such a shrew of a wife? She had been pondering it all evening. But that wasn't the only thing she'd been wondering about. Mrs. Davis had suddenly become cordial and polite. In fact, she could even go so far as to say Nellie Davis was being … *nice?*

"I think I'll go put the coffee on. Miss James, have you had enough?" Mrs. Davis asked sweetly.

Summer forced herself not to audibly gulp at

the woman's syrupy tone. Something *had* to be wrong! Her eyes darted about the table. Abbey and Charlotte were giggling as they talked about something Milly Brown had said to their father, while Mrs. Davis continued to look at her with a silly smile plastered on her usually pinched face. Summer knew a fake smile when she saw one. None of the evening seemed real, and she began to seriously wonder if any of it was.

But then, this wasn't Winslow, and it wasn't New Orleans. Maybe folks out here got over things quickly. Like venomous snakes that suddenly decided they no longer liked the taste of plump little mice …

Summer did gulp at that. It was never a good thing to be a mouse in a snake's nest; no matter how pleasant the accommodations or polite the company, one knew one could all too easily become a snack ...

"Is something wrong, Miss James?" Mrs. Davis asked.

Summer forced another smile. "No, nothing's wrong. But I really do need to be going…"

"Nonsense! You can't travel at night in your condition!" Mr. Davis huffed. "What if something happened? You'd never make it back to town on foot."

"I … well, I…" Summer began.

"You can stay here!" Mr. Davis chortled. "Folks in these parts do it all the time. Your ma … I mean, your soon-to-be-ma … she knows you're here. Let that Clayton come fetch you in the morning. It's too cold for any of us to be out this late. Besides, you know what they say – absence makes the heart grow fonder!" He slapped the table again and burst into laughter.

Summer tried not to grimace. The thought of spending the night with the Davises made her head hurt. Pain shot straight to her temples, and she closed her eyes against it as Mrs. Davis disappeared into the kitchen. In between dinner and dessert, Mr. Davis continued to smack the table every time he talked, his dutiful daughters both laughing along with anything he said.

Oh, Clayton, Summer inwardly sighed to herself as Mrs. Davis finally returned to the kitchen with cake and coffee. *Where are you?*

Clayton rode down the street to the stage and telegraph office to see if Sam Olsen, who ran the place, was still there. Unfortunately, the office was closed. He groaned, turned his horse and headed back the other way, slowing only enough to turn down another street that would take him to the main road out of town and home.

How could she leave? Had Spencer driven her to town? No, how could he? Spencer probably couldn't even get out of bed – he was still sleeping when Clayton had gotten up, and he didn't look so good. He had meant to ride straight to Doc's as soon as he got to town.

But the moment Clayton saw Summer sitting at the kitchen table peeling apples, everything changed. The brutality of what he'd seen the last few weeks flooded his mind. Two entire families slaughtered, not fifty miles from Nowhere. The women, the children … what sort of evil possessed a man to do such things? Now he knew how Red Ned got his name – he left a trail of blood wherever he went, and all for a few horses and supplies. Why didn't the man just take what he needed and leave the settlers alone? But no, he had to leave his mark behind.

Clayton vowed that he would retire as sheriff and go back to farming. But before he did, he'd make sure Red Ned was brought to justice. He didn't have to go out with every posse – he could make do in town and wire a few U.S. Marshals to widen the search. From the looks of it, Red Ned had headed south. He decided to also wire his Uncle Harlan in Clear Creek, it being the largest town south of Nowhere. Besides, Uncle Harlan would have his hide if he didn't give him the heads-up that a murdering varmint was heading back his way.

By the time Clayton made it home, it had started to snow. He put his horse in the barn but didn't unsaddle him, just in case he needed to leave right away. He headed into the house to find his mother and see what she knew about Summer.

She was sitting at the kitchen table, her face puffy, eyes red from crying. "Ma? What happened?"

His mother looked up at him. "Clayton! Oh Clayton, is Summer with you?"

"No, I was hoping she was with you …"

"I can't find her anywhere! And Spencer's been sick all day – I've been afraid to leave him!"

Clayton stormed across the kitchen to the small office Summer used as her bedroom. Nothing seemed out of place, except that she wasn't in it. But as he looked around he noticed some of her things were gone: the hair ribbons he'd bought for her, the book of poetry she liked, even that ragged dress she'd arrived in town wearing. He'd swear it was hanging up on a hook near the window last night after she'd put her nightdress on. He closed his eyes as his hands clenched at his sides. "Summer …," he groaned.

"I looked everywhere for her," his mother said from behind him. "The barn, the orchards, I found no trace! And what's worse, her satchel's gone! I know she kept it under the bed, and it's gone, Clayton! Gone!"

He turned to his mother and quickly took her in his arms as she wept anew. How could that girl have done such a thing? What could have possibly happened to make her leave so suddenly? Surely his behavior that morning hadn't been enough to drive her away?

Or was it? She was an orphan, and he knew her biggest fear was rejection, abandonment. Had she misinterpreted his actions? Did she think he didn't want to marry her anymore? He and Spencer *had* been gone for quite a spell, but the job required it. In fact, it was part of the reason he'd decided to go back to apple farming …

"Clayton, what are we going to do?" his mother cried.

"First, I need to figure out how she got herself off this farm. Someone had to have helped her."

His mother sniffed back her tears, looked up and studied him a moment. "Yes, you're right. None of our horses are missing, and the wagon's still here. But who?"

"You didn't hear anything? See anyone?"

She shook her head as she sniffed back more tears. "I was in the barn for quite a while after you left. You'd upset me so ..."

He drew her back into his chest and held her there. "Ah, Ma, I'm sorry. But during this last search, me and the posse found things no man ought to lay eyes on, not even a lawman. It made me think, and I decided to make some changes. I'm sorry I didn't tell you about them before I left in such a hurry." He loosened his grip to let him look her in the eye. "Old Man Johnson's agreed to give the orchards back once the lease is up. It's become too much for him, and I'm ready to get back to farming. But I don't have time to explain now – I've got to find Summer! If she left on the two o'clock stage, she's got half a day's head start on me."

"Oh, Clayton, do you really think she left town?"

He pulled the note from his pocket and handed it to her. His mother gasped when she read it. "You can't let her leave, Clayton!"

"I don't plan to, even if I have to chase that stage all night. They had to have stopped over at the Gundersons'. I'll saddle Spencer's horse and head out right away." He took the note back and stuffed it in his pocket. "Fix me a sandwich or something, will you?"

His mother nodded as she wiped her tears. "There's no good reason why Summer would have left – none. She seemed so happy here!"

"Don't worry, Ma. I'll bring her back if it's the last thing I do."

Of course, he had to find her first.

Summer lay in the bed she was sharing with Abbey and let go a weary sigh. Before the Davis sisters fell asleep, she'd had to listen to Charlotte carry on about the horrors of living in Nowhere, prattling on for what seemed like an eternity. Thankfully, sleep finally overtook both sisters, to leave her alone with her thoughts, disturbing though they were. If she didn't know any better, she'd say Charlotte was trying to dissuade her from staying in Nowhere. Which perhaps she was, but how could she tell?

All she knew was how badly she wanted to see Clayton, talk with him, tell him how she felt. Tell him she loved him. She hoped and prayed that when she did see him, the fear usually so quick to render her speechless would remain silent for once. She *had* to tell him!

Abbey suddenly laughed in her sleep, turned over, and flopped one arm over Summer's belly. Summer winced, sighed, then did her best to pick up the girl's arm and move it. At least she was sharing a bed with Abbey and not Charlotte – otherwise, that girl might *still* be talking! *Clayton, why didn't you come for me?* she sighed to herself.

But wait a minute – why *hadn't* he? They'd left the note at the sheriff's office, and he had to have gone there at some point during the day. Surely he'd read it by now! So why didn't he come get her earlier and take her home? He couldn't have known she had decided to leave and begun to pack her satchel ... unless he'd gone back to the farm first. Would he be angry that she'd done so? What did Mrs. Riley think?

Guilt rose like bile in her throat. Poor Mrs. Riley – did the woman think she'd run away? But no, Mrs. Riley had to have seen her with Charlotte as they left the farm.

Oh, what was she to think? Well, other than the obvious ... Clayton hadn't come for her after reading the note because he *had* decided not to marry her. Her heart sank with the thought. *Oh, Lord, no! Help me to show him I love him! Help me get back to the farm first thing in the morning!*

But what good would it do? If he'd wanted her back at the farm, she'd be there. He surely would have come for her after reading the note and taken her home.

Home ... where would her home be now? What was she to do? She'd been so angry that afternoon, so confident in her spur-of-the-moment plan to go to Doc and Milly's and stay there a few days until she decided what to do.

"I have no money," she whispered to herself as reality hit hard and fast. "I have no family... no place to go and no one to see."

The numbness came out of nowhere. It encircled her heart and mind with a force so powerful, so deadly, that in the past it would have alarmed her. But not this time – this time she welcomed it. She hoped it would give her the strength to do what she knew she had to.

Leave.

FOURTEEN

Clayton stood in shock as the stagecoach driver folded his arms over his chest and spat. "I'm tellin' ya, Sheriff, there ain't no woman on this stage by the name of Summer James. There ain't no women, period – them's all men asleep in there!"

He'd ridden through the dark with nothing but the bright moonlight shining on the snow-covered ground, and arrived at the Gundersons' stage stop well after midnight. He immediately found the driver and woke him up. Of course at that point he probably woke up the entire establishment, but he didn't care. He had to find Summer!

"You mean there wasn't a woman on this stage at all?" Clayton asked in disbelief.

"That's what I said! Just three men. Maybe she planned on taking the morning stage."

"Morning stage!"

"Yep, ten o'clock."

"Good God!" Clayton tried to collect himself as he calculated what time he'd seen Summer the day before. "No, it's not possible – she couldn't have left on the ten o'clock stage."

"Hafta agree with ya there."

Clayton stared at the driver. He was tired, he was hungry, and he wasn't sure he heard him right. "What did you say? How could you know she didn't take the ten o'clock stage?"

"Because it ain't left yet. This here's the two o'clock stage, there's a ten o'clock stage leavin' Nowhere in the morning."

"Today?"

The driver spat again. "Yep." He scratched at his long underwear. "Now if ya don't mind, I need to get me some shuteye. Dawn comes mighty early, ya know." He stomped off to resume his interrupted sleep.

Clayton stood with his mouth hanging open like a dote, and stared at the wall. She hadn't left; she couldn't have. But if she didn't leave Nowhere, where *did* she go?

He rubbed his tired eyes with his hands. He'd be a fool to try to ride back now. The horse needed food and rest, and so did he. He'd have to get at least a few hours sleep before heading out again. He went outside, led the horse to the barn and took care of him. Then he returned to the house, found the food Mrs. Gunderson had set out for him, ate, and then after finding the blanket she left, bedded himself down in the parlor.

But sleep didn't come so easy to Clayton – there were too many unanswered questions, one in particular. *Who* did Summer leave the farm with?

Clayton suddenly groaned when he realized

it could only be one person, or in this case four -
the Davis family. Who else would have her and
not let any of his family know about it? "Lord
have mercy!" he spoke to the dark. "Charlotte,
you scheming little minx, what are you trying to
pull now?"

"I'm so sorry none of it worked out for you,
but I'm sure you'll find a job in Clear Creek."
Mr. Davis told her as he helped her climb into
the morning stage. "Why, that little town has the
prettiest hotel in Oregon! Big, too! I'll be sure to
send a telegraph to Mr. Van Cleet the hotel
owner. I've had dealings with him a time or
two. Nice fella."

Charlotte and Abbey had woken before dawn
to Summer's soft weeping, and both sisters did
their best to console her. Charlotte even told
Summer she should wait and talk to Clayton
before she left, but Summer wouldn't hear it.
She was determined to leave, and was now
convinced the girl was only trying to help her.
After all, if Charlotte wanted to truly get rid of
her, she'd have all but shoved her onto the
afternoon stage the day before, but she didn't.
Instead, she took her home to have tea and
biscuits with her sister. Now she was trying to
get her to wait until Clayton showed up to speak
with him. But as the morning waned on, it
became quite apparent that Clayton Riley wasn't
showing up any time soon.

"Thank you, Mr. Davis. I'll repay you as soon as I can," Summer told him. At breakfast Abbey sweet-talked her father into lending the stage fare. As she didn't have enough money to go back to New Orleans, and wasn't about to ask Mr. Davis for the money to do so, Summer took Charlotte's suggestion to head south and accepted fare to Clear Creek.

The best thing about it was she wouldn't have to face Clayton – wouldn't have to hear him tell her he no longer wanted her, wouldn't have to suffer that humiliation in front of his brother and Mrs. Riley. Maybe she was being a coward, but she didn't care. She didn't even care that she was leaving with nothing but the clothes on her back – that's how she'd arrived, after all. She just wanted to go, as soon as possible.

The ten o'clock stage lurched forward. She waved numbly to the Davis family as they huddled in a little group to stay warm. Even Mrs. Davis came along and sadly waved her goodbyes to the sound of jangling harness and the slap of leather reins.

As the stage headed down Nowhere's main street Summer turned from the window, faced forward and took a deep breath. She didn't feel guilty for leaving without a word. She didn't feel anything but the numbing effects of her weeping earlier that morning, at the cold hard fact that Clayton hadn't come for her.

Maybe Charlotte was right. Maybe she should have talked with him. But didn't she wait until the last possible minute before it came time to leave? And *still* he hadn't come.

Summer, the only passenger on the stage, took advantage of the dark solitude of the empty coach and wept what few tears she had left.

Clayton left at dawn. He was furious with himself as he rode out, but figured if he hurried he would come upon the stage not more than an hour or so after it left town. But as the morning wore on and he drew closer to Nowhere, he began wondering why he hadn't see any sign of it. Could it be running late, or perhaps had some trouble along the way?

A wave of panic gripped him as he thought of Red Ned and his gang. But Ned, in all probability, was heading south to Clear Creek. The outlaw would become his uncle's problem. As soon as he had Summer safely back home, he'd try and remember to wire Uncle Harlan like he'd planned.

But first, he had to find her.

Clayton reached Nowhere and went straight to his office. He burst through the door to find Billy leaned back in his chair with his feet propped on the desk talking with Doc. "Doc! Have you been out to the farm? Is Spencer all right?"

"Whoa there, son. Yep, I've already been out there and back this morning. He'll be fine – nasty bump he got, but he'll pull through and be ready for Christmas morning. Sorry I couldn't make it out last night, but I was back at the Colson farm again. Mrs. Colson's got herself a new bouncing baby boy. Six young'uns – that poor woman has her hands full!"

Clayton nodded in acknowledgement then pushed his hat off his forehead. "Were either of you here when the stage left this morning?"

"I was still out at your place," Doc told him. "In fact, I just got back into town."

Billy took his feet off the desk, pushed the chair back and stood. "I was down at the livery stable. My horse done threw a shoe this mornin'."

"Did either of you see Charlotte Davis in town with Summer?" Clayton asked.

"I didn't," Billy said. Doc shook his head.

Clayton closed his eyes a moment in frustration. He then opened them and looked at Billy. "I need your horse."

"My horse? What fer?"

"I need to catch that stage."

"But boss, how do ya even know if she's on it?"

"Billy's right, Clayton. If you think your little gal was with Charlotte Davis, then she might still be there. Why don't you go on out to the Davis place and check first before you go galloping after that stage?"

"Yeah, ya might chase the stage down only to find Miss James ain't on it," Billy added.

Clayton groaned. "You're both right. I guess I'm plumb tuckered out and not thinking straight at this point. Heck, I didn't even see the stage when I was coming back from the

Gundersons'."

"Well, boss, it wasn't headin' that way."

What do you mean? Where is it, then?"

"The ten o'clock stage was goin' to Clear Creek."

Clayton took his hat off, hit his leg with it, then slammed the desk with his fist. How could he have forgotten a detail like that?

Doc laughed. "Son, what you need is some marrying! Why don't I go round up the preacher while you go round up your pretty little gal, then you can get down to business?"

"Yeah," Billy agreed. "Won't she make for a nice Christmas present?"

"Christmas?" Clayton barked.

"Well, yeah, boss. Today's Christmas Eve."

Christmas Eve? Clayton couldn't believe it! Where had the time gone? Had they really been searching for that no-good varmint Red Ned all month? Apparently so. And he was more tuckered out than he first thought, if he didn't even know what day it was.

Furthermore, he hadn't given a single thought to the holiday! He wasn't even sure if there was a tree up in the house ... probably not, as he and Spencer had usually been the ones to go out and find one! Why hadn't his mother said anything?

Because you haven't been around to say anything to, you idiot! He rubbed his forehead and let his hand slide down his face as he groaned. No gifts. No tree. No preparation whatsoever. *And now, possibly no wife ...*

First things first. "I'm heading over to the

Davises', then. If Summer's not there, I'll go after that stage."

"Whatcha want me to do, boss?"

Clayton looked at Billy, grateful for his help. "If you've got the time, get my mother a Christmas tree."

"How can I help?" Doc asked.

Clayton's eyes flashed with determination. "Fetch the preacher. We're gonna have a wedding." And with that, he stormed out of the sheriff's office in search of his future bride.

Clayton mounted Billy's horse and headed for the Davises' house. Their place was at least a mile out of town in the opposite direction the stage would have gone, and he seethed knowing Charlotte may have been up to no good.

But what if he was wrong? What if there was no ill intent involved? He'd best calm himself down, lest he be tempted to break through the front door and storm into the house. What would Summer think of him then? On the other hand, maybe barreling into the Davis house, throwing her over his shoulder and carrying all the way to the preacher's was what he needed to do – prove to her that he wasn't messing around, that he meant business!

No, not business. Love.

He slowed the horse to a trot as he got closer to his destination. He didn't want Summer to see him angry, and decided the best thing to do would be to gather her up, get her home, and get ready for the upcoming holiday. They could be married that evening and wake up Christmas morning as husband and wife.

Clayton smiled at the thought. She might fuss a little over not having a wedding dress and all, but she could always wear his mother's red dress. She sure looked mighty pretty in it the day she'd had it on. In fact, the sight had taken his breath away. He knew why his mother had kept it, knew the story behind it.

Clayton's smile broadened as he rode up to the Davises' hitching post and dismounted. He was much calmer now, thinking about what he wanted to tell Summer as soon as the door opened and he caught sight of her. He went through the gate, marched up to the front door, took a deep breath and knocked.

Nellie Davis answered the door. "Why, Clayton Riley, whatever brings you here?" she asked innocently.

His resolve to stay calm was immediately tested. "I've come for Summer. Where is she?"

"Summer? Oh, you mean that Miss James?"

"Of course that's who I mean. Where is she?"

"Well, now, don't get upset. How should I know where she is?"

"You mean she's not here?" Clayton barked.

"Certainly not! Why on earth would she be?"

Clayton stared at her as the first traces of panic began to grip him. "You mean to tell me she's not here at all? She didn't come here yesterday?"

Mrs. Davis pursed her lips together before she spoke. "No. Why would she?"

Clayton's hands balled into fists. Now where was he to look? What could have happened to her?

"Who's that at the door, Mother?" a voice called.

"It's Clayton – he's come looking for that Miss James."

Charlotte pushed past her mother as she wrapped a shawl around her shoulders. "Why, Clayton, what a surprise!" She quickly turned to her mother. "Why don't you go back inside and close the door? The house will get cold with it hanging wide open like this!"

Mrs. Davis smiled sweetly and nodded in agreement. "You two have yourselves a nice little visit. Come by again soon, Clayton. Christmas, maybe?"

"Don't count on it," he said as he glared down at her.

Mrs. Davis's face took on its usual pinched expression as she forced a smile and closed the door.

"Where's Summer?" he asked through clenched teeth as he turned his attention to Charlotte.

"Summer? Why, I have no idea. Isn't she at home ... oh dear ..."

"Oh dear what?"

"Well ... you see, there *was* talk that she left. I thought I was hearing things – you know how rumors get started ..."

"What talk?" he demanded.

"Down at the mercantile, Mrs. Quinn might have mentioned that she heard Miss James had had enough of this town, and was going to leave. In fact, she was so desperate to leave she … well … she…"

"She what?" Clayton spat.

"She didn't even wait for the stage, she rode out with some stranger."

Clayton's eyes narrowed to slits. "Is that the truth, Charlotte?"

"Oh, now, Clayton, I got the story secondhand. How should I know if there's any truth to it? And who knows who Mrs. Quinn heard it from."

It was all Clayton could do to keep from growling at her. Who in Sam blazes would have taken Summer and ridden out of town with her? She *had* to have taken the stage! Clayton finally did growl as he turned on his boot heel to leave.

Charlotte reached out and grabbed his coat. "Clayton!"

He spun to her, his face covered in barely controlled rage.

Charlotte took a deep breath as she took in his expression. "It never would have worked between you. What are you so angry about it? I think it's a blessing in disguise she's gone."

"A blessing for who, Charlotte? For you? Are you thinking that just because Summer's gone, if indeed she really *is* gone, I'd marry you now?"

Her mouth fell open in shock. "Clayton Riley, how could you say such a thing?"

"Easily enough. I know you too well."

"Now, Clayton, you'll get over her. She wasn't good enough for you anyway. Why, the girl was dull and ugly. I'll never understand why you even considered marrying her! Besides, you said so yourself – you weren't the one that sent away for her in the first place!"

Clayton's eyes narrowed to slits. "What did you do with her?"

Charlotte backed up a step at his tone. "Why, nothing! What makes you think I had anyth–"

"If there were any strangers in town, Billy would have told me."

Charlotte swallowed hard and pulled the shawl more tightly about her. "I think I'd … better go inside before I catch my death of cold …"

Clayton took a step toward her. "Where is she?"

"Now Clayton, I really do have to be getting inside …"

Clayton reached out, grabbed her by the upper arms and pulled her to him. Her expression immediately changed to dreamy adoration. "Why, Clayton Riley, you're holding me in a most improper way. Why, if my daddy saw us like this, he'd get out the shotgun and insist we marry." Her tone was sugary sweet, almost sickening.

Now Clayton knew, *knew* Charlotte had done something to Summer. "Not if I'm arresting you, he won't." That cooled her ardor a little. "Tell me what you did with her, Charlotte. Tell me now."

Charlotte tried to take control of the situation

again, by putting her arms around him and pulling her body against his. "Don't you see, Clayton?" she cooed. "She was never meant for you. She left because she knew you didn't want her – knew it the moment you didn't come for her. That's why she left." Tears formed in her eyes and she held him ever tighter. "Kiss me, Clayton. Kiss me and tell me we'll be married now. I don't want anybody else! I'll die if I have to marry anyone except you!"

Clayton was about to comment in the negative and begin peeling Charlotte off of him when the front door opened. Mr. Davis stepped out, shotgun in hand. "What's going on out here? Mrs. Davis told me you were compromising my little girl! Said she saw you do it through the window!"

Charlotte's face lit up and her arms tightened as Clayton quickly glanced to the window. The lace curtain fell back into place before he could catch a glimpse of Charlotte's scheming mother. Obviously she'd sent Mr. Davis out with the news *and* the gun. "Mr. Davis, it's nothing of the sort!" Clayton growled.

"I think it is! Just look at the way you're holding on to my little girl!"

"Holding on to *her*?" Clayton quickly held up both hands as his face twisted in disbelief. Charlotte had her arms locked around him in a vise grip, her cheek against his chest and a delighted look on her face, like a child who'd just been given a pony.

"There's only one thing to do in a case like this," Mrs. Davis cried as she shoved her way through the door past her husband. "He's going to have to marry her!"

"Are you out of your mind?" Clayton spat. "I am not marrying Charlotte!"

"Clayton! Don't you love me?" Charlotte wailed.

"No!"

"Why, you low-down scum!" Mr. Davis bellowed, raising the shotgun higher. "First you break the heart of that pretty little gal we sent off this morning, and now my Charlotte's! You aren't fit to be sheriff!"

Clayton stiffened at his words. Charlotte squeezed him tighter in response, so tight he wondered if he'd be able to breathe. "Wait ... what gal you sent off this morning?"

But Mr. Davis was past the point of listening. "You're not fit to be sheriff – and not only that, you're not fit for my little girl!"

"Daddy!" Charlotte cried as she loosened her grip on Clayton and turned toward her father. "He is so, and you'd best tie him up and go fetch the preacher quick-like!"

"Oh, good grief." Clayton moaned as he rubbed his temples with his fingers. "Dear Lord, make it stop ...."

"I'll get some rope!" Mrs. Davis cried as Charlotte once again tightened her arms around him.

"I always respected you, Sheriff, but after this morning I see you're nothing but a cad." Mr. Davis said as he took a threatening step forward and raised the shotgun higher still.

Clayton put both hands in the air. "Put that

gun away, Mr. Davis," he told him sternly.

"Are you gonna do the right thing and marry my little girl?"

"No."

"Then you leave me no choice."

"Daddy!" Charlotte cried, "For God's sake, don't shoot him! He's the only one I want!"

It was at this point that Abbey came out to see what all the fuss was. "Daddy, what are you doing?"

"Thank God," Clayton mumbled to himself. "Abbey, where's Summer?"

"We put her on the stage this morning. She's heading to Clear Creek."

"Abbey!" Charlotte screeched.

Clayton ignored her. "Abbey, did she want to leave?"

Charlotte shot her sister a warning glare as Mr. Davis lowered the gun a little.

"I don't know. We all thought you'd come for her last night, but you didn't. Then we thought you'd at least show up this morning, but ..."

"I didn't know she was here. I didn't know where she was. Heck, I chased down the stage and spent the night at the Gundersons' thinking I'd find her there."

"What?" Mr. Davis barked. "But she left you a note telling you she was here!"

"She left me a note telling me she was leaving."

Mr. Davis lowered the shotgun. "Charlotte ..." he said warningly.

Charlotte audibly gulped and slowly turned

to face her father. "Yes, daddy?" she replied weakly.

Her father's voice was low and suspicious. "What mischief have you and your mother been up to? Who wrote that note?"

"Er ... well ..."

"*Get* your hands off the sheriff!" Mr. Davis demanded. "And get inside the house! I'll be dealing with you later!"

Charlotte gritted her teeth and let go of Clayton. She glared at him, then at her father. She then spun to Clayton. "It'll never work, Clayton Riley, mark my words. You're a fool. You pout over Sarah for years, then go and take the first little harlot that comes along when you could have had me–"

"Charlotte!" Mr. Davis yelled, his face turning red as raw steak. "I did *not* tell you to talk – I told you to *get in that house*! NOW!"

Charlotte's mouth snapped shut, and with a look of betrayal on her face she stomped into the house, shoving Abbey out of the way as she did.

Mr. Davis watched her go before he gave Clayton a sheepish look. "I am awful sorry, Sheriff. I had no idea my ..." He shook his head. ".. my own wife and daughter would act so low-down and trifling."

"It's all right, Mr. Davis. Just do us both a favor and keep a tighter rein on your family from now on."

"Oh, I will. I will," Mr. Davis assured him. "And if you don't mind me saying so, that little gal of yours loves you. Abbey here tells me she cried most of the night when you didn't show. The only thing I could think of that might help her broken heart would be to get her out of Nowhere and have herself a fresh start someplace else. I apologize for that – clearly it was the wrong thing to do. But at least now you know where she is."

Clayton sighed wearily. "Well, I'm much obliged to Abbey for telling me."

"I'm glad one of my daughters has some sense," Mr. Davis opined.

A loud wail came from the other side of the door. Abbey glanced at it, then looked to her father and rolled her eyes. "Daddy …"

"I'll take care of your sister – you just go on inside now." He turned back to Clayton. "I can't say how sorry I am – and rest assured, I'll make sure my daughter – and my wife – never pull a stunt like this again." He shook his head in frustration. "Go get your bride, Sheriff. She's a much better match for you than Charlotte will ever be. Besides, you're deserving of a good woman after what you've been through."

Clayton let a smile form on his face. He reached out and shook Mr. Davis's hand. "Thank you, Mr. Davis, and Merry Christmas."

Mr. Davis smiled broadly. "Merry Christmas, son. And speaking of which, you'd best go fetch your Christmas bride!"

"I'll do that." Clayton said with a wink. He untied his horse, mounted, and went to get his Christmas present – or rather, bride. But at this point, he almost felt he needed to wrap her up with ribbon and keep her under the tree until they could be married. At least that way he couldn't lose her again!

FIFTEEN

Summer awoke at the first stage stop several hours out of Nowhere with a kink in her neck, a hitch in her side and a sting in her eyes. She'd cried herself to sleep earlier and now felt completely wrung out, like a dishrag that had seen better days. She would need help down from the stage, and hoped the driver remembered her injured foot. He had watched Mr. Davis hand her the pair of crutches before they left town. They were on the seat opposite her, and she stiffly reached for them.

She heard the driver climb down. He opened the door, tipped his hat, and helped her out. "We're changing horses. You've got twenty minutes before we head out again."

She nodded her thanks, took her crutches and headed for the nearest building. It was almost the only building, that and a barn, but so long as they had water and a little something to eat she'd be fine. Abbey had given her some money for the trip, at least enough to survive on until she got to Clear Creek. After that she was on God's good humor – that and the man called

Van Cleet.

She hobbled inside and waited for her eyes to adjust to the dim light before searching the room for signs of life. There were none, except for a man passed out at one table. An empty whiskey bottle and glass sat near his head, which rested on one arm. He began to snore loudly, and she felt her spine stiffen against the sound.

"Hello?" she said weakly. "Is anybody here?" She glanced around once more, but there was still no one else. She briefly wondered if the snoring man was the proprietor, then thought better of it. Why would the owner of the establishment be passed out if he knew a stage was coming in? Or she did have to remind herself, once again, that this was not New Orleans.

The man mumbled something into his arm, snorted, then began snoring again.

Summer sighed and went behind the small bar to see if there was a pitcher of water. She found a clean glass, at least, but nothing but alcohol to drink. Maybe there was a kitchen out back, or at least a pump.

With the aid of her crutches she made her way down a hall and, sure enough, found the kitchen. "Oh, thank the Lord," she said to herself as she spied a pitcher of water on the counter. She just hoped she could find another clean glass, as she'd left the one she found in the other room. She did, poured herself some water, and was just about to take a drink when she heard it.

A pain-filled groan.

Summer froze. She looked right, then left, but saw nothing.

The groan came again. This time she followed the sound, looked to the left and down … and dropped the glass. It shattered as it hit the floor. "Oh, God!"

A man lay on the floor in a pool of blood.

Summer's hands flew to her mouth to stifle a panicked scream. What should she do? Where was everybody? She quickly got her wits about her and hobbled down the hall to the front room and out the door.

By the time she was back outside, tears were streaming down her face from the horrible sight of the dying man in the kitchen. "Help!" she cried. "Come quickly!"

But no one answered.

She looked in all directions for the driver, then noticed the same team of horses was still hitched to the wagon. Nothing had been done yet to change them out. What was going on?

"Help! Someone come here! There's a man inside that's bleeding!" But still no answer. She began to panic as she made her way behind the stage to the other side, where she promptly screamed first, then fainted.

She fell next to the driver, who lay on the ground with his throat slit ear to ear.

Clayton rode Billy's horse hard. If he hurried, he could catch the stage before it left the first stop. They'd change horses there, and that would give him time to catch up.

The wind was cold but the sun was bright. The snow still on the ground wasn't enough to slow him down, and for that he was grateful. In the distance he could see clouds forming; they'd be overhead by nightfall. He smiled at the thought of a white Christmas. He sure hoped Billy was able to find a tree! How much more perfect could the evening be? A tree, snowfall, his beautiful Summer in his arms and a proposal on his lips.

He'd see them married before the day was out, that was for sure! He wasn't about to let her slip away from him again, unintentional or not! He was going to tell her he loved her as soon as he found her. Then he was going to kiss her senseless – kiss her so long and hard her knees gave out and she couldn't breathe, kiss her until there was no doubt as to how he felt about her. Then he'd make her his wife and show her how he *really* felt!

Clayton smiled at the thought and kicked Billy's horse into a faster gallop.

Summer opened her eyes slowly. Her foot hurt, but not as much as her head. She remembered going outside, trying to find the driver, and then … she'd found him all right – dead as a doornail in a pool of blood like the man in the kitchen.

Her stomach lurched at the thought, and she tried to stand up, only to discover she was tied to a chair. She automatically screamed, but the sound was cut off; she'd been gagged as well. She froze, tried to calm herself against the mind-numbing fear threatening to take control. What was going on? Who had done such horrible things?

She realized she was back in the main room of the stage stop, and remembered the man passed out on the table. She turned her head, and he was still there, snoring more softly now. Fear took hold at that point and she sobbed into the gag.

She must have made enough noise to attract attention, as voices suddenly sounded from the kitchen. Boot-steps followed, and soon two men entered the room. One wore an eye patch. He looked her up and down then laughed. "Ya see? Toldja she wouldn't be out fer long! Now we have some fun, huh?" He laughed again and hit his companion on the back.

"But Sam's still out cold."

"Too bad fer Sam – more fer us! I get 'er first!" The man came up to the chair and pulled out a huge knife. Summer again tried to scream as tears poured from her eyes.

"But Ned, we need to get the horses. There's nothing else here."

"You git the stinkin' horses an' then wake Sam up. Soon as I'm done, we'll leave."

"Now wait a minute, what about me?"

The one with the eye-patch spun to him. "If yer so worried 'bout getting them horses together, then go do it! While yer brother's wakin' up, ya can have yer turn with the girl. 'Til then, git!"

The other man grumbled, then turned and stomped out to where the stage waited.

Summer began to tremble. She couldn't think, could barely breathe!

The man snarled as he looked her up and down. "What happened to yer foot?" he asked as he leaned down and cut the ropes that tied her ankles together and to the chair. She instinctively kicked at him with her good foot, but it only made him laugh.

He leaned over her again and cut the bonds lashing her wrists together behind the chair. "Ya wanna fight me, huh? Think ya can take down the famous Red Ned?" He laughed again, picked her up and threw her over one shoulder like a sack of grain, then sauntered his way down the hall, kicking doors open while he ignored her struggles.

Red Ned! The same outlaw Clayton had been searching for all this time! Summer's body froze with fear. She was surely going to die, and even though she knew what was to come, her greatest regret was her own foolishness. She regretted leaving Nowhere. She regretted letting her anger get the best of her. She regretted trusting Charlotte Davis – of all people! – and letting her talk her into getting on that blasted stage. But most of all, as the infamous Red Ned threw her down upon the bed he'd finally found, she regretted never telling Clayton Riley she loved him.

"Now lessee, how d'ya want it? Ah, I know – *alive!* That way, you'll remember who hadja right before ya die ..."

Summer knew she should fight him and try to escape, but fear had frozen every muscle. Besides, how could she run? She could barely walk yet. She closed her eyes, trying to think. Red Ned whistled while he took off his gun belt, then began to casually remove his shirt.

An idea came to her, hard enough to kick her muscles into gear. She rolled to the side, off the bed, and scooted under it. She'd done that countless times while growing up in the orphanage – it would slow things down, let her buy a few moments to think of something else. The longer it kept her alive, the better. *Oh, Lord, help me!* she prayed silently.

But Red Ned didn't grab her and drag her out from under the bed as she expected. Instead he threw back his head and laughed. "Ya think that's gonna help ya? I can just throw the bed aside and take ya on the floor. That whatcha want?" He laughed again as he walked toward the bed.

In fact, he was laughing so hard, he didn't hear the man enter the room behind him.

Neither could Summer, but she saw him, and recognized the boots. It was actually a good thing she was still gagged – Red Ned couldn't hear her muffled squeal as she watched Clayton Riley boldly step into the room, spin the outlaw around and punch him square in the gut before delivering an uppercut to his jaw.

The outlaw reeled from the blow and

tumbled back upon the bed. The impact smacked Summer's jaw against the floor, and she lay stunned for a moment as the two men began to fight.

Well, for the most part only one of them was fighting. "That's for mistreating my bride!" she heard Clayton growl before he punched Red Ned in the face again. "And this is for what you intended to do!" Another punch. "And this one's for the settlers you murdered!" Another blow, and another, and Red Ned was down, his face now an unrecognizable, bloodied mess a few feet away from her. She watched numbly as Clayton dragged him to the side of the room, then quickly came to the bed and did as Red Ned had threatened – flipping the bed up and away from her.

"Summer!" he cried as he bent down and took her in his arms. "Honey, are you okay? Did he hurt you?" He removed the gag, tossed it aside and took her face in his hands. "Talk to me, Summer, say something!"

She looked at him, then glanced at Red Ned, or what was left of him. She opened her mouth, but only a whimper came out. Her body began to shake and heave with silent sobs.

"It's all right, you're safe now. He can't hurt you anymore." Clayton kissed the top of her head and held her tightly against him, as on the first day she saw him. The day he'd accidentally shot her. She wondered what would have happened if he hadn't. There would have been no reason for her to stay if she thought he didn't want her. He might have packed her up and sent her on her way. Or, more likely, she would have misinterpreted one of his silences and let her fear drive her away from him ... just as she had this morning.

She gazed up into his emerald eyes, and again tried to speak, but still no words came out.

He looked deep into her own eyes. "It's okay. I know how scared you are. It's okay if you can't talk yet. It happens."

Red Ned groaned.

Clayton glanced at him then quickly gave his attention back to her. "I have to secure him, and then I'm taking you out of here. You're safe now – he can't hurt you anymore, understand?"

She shook her head. "Clayton ..." she barely whispered. "There ... are two other ..."

He smiled and held her face between his hands. "Not anymore there isn't. One lit on out of here as soon as he saw me ride up. The other, I've already tied to his chair – not that he noticed, being passed out drunk. I don't care about either of them – this one's the big catch."

He lowered his face to hers. "I'm going to take care of him, and then the dead men. Then ..." He was so close now she could feel the warm brush of his breath against her skin. "Summer, Summer James, I love you." He didn't wait for her to say anything. He kissed her, kissed her with all the pent-up longing of his lonely heart.

Summer had never been kissed before, and didn't know what it would be like. It wasn't gentle – it was pure possession, and she thought she might faint from the power of it. She didn't want it to end – ever!

Unfortunately, Red Ned groaned again, as he began to regain consciousness. Clayton was sorely tempted to shoot the bandit just so he could keep kissing Summer! But no, Red Ned had caused too much trouble for him, and Clayton vowed to see him brought to justice. Besides, shooting off a gun in such close quarters would probably spoil the moment for Summer ...

Clayton got up, and pulled Summer up with him. He carried her to the other side of the room and set her down in the chair. He kissed her again, more gently this time. "This'll just take a moment," he whispered, and turned to secure the infamous Red Ned.

The stage rolled into Nowhere just after sundown. Billy ran out of the sheriff's office in time to see Clayton climb down from the driver's seat. He wearily went around to the back and motioned for his deputy to join him. "Help me get these two men locked up."

"Jumpin' Jehosaphat, is that Red Ned?" Billy asked as he noted one of the men that Clayton had tied to their horses and led behind the stagecoach all the way back to Nowhere. Neither outlaw looked too good, but the other one's face was only covered with dried vomit. Red Ned's face looked more like a badly butchered cut of beef ...

"Yes it is, and one of his henchmen. Let's get them into the cell. I've got to get Summer home."

"Who's the other one?" he inquired as Clayton cut both outlaws loose and watched them fall to the ground. They both moaned as they hit the dirt.

"The other one is Samuel Cooke. He escaped from prison a year ago along with his brother Jack. Jack got away, but I'm sure he'll get rounded up soon enough."

"I can't believe we've been after this scum for so long, and here you go and bring him in singlehanded! How'd you do it?" Billy asked, enthralled.

Clayton's face was grim. "Let's just say Ned let himself get distracted."

"Well, don't that beat all!" Billy said with a grin as they dragged the outlaws into the jail and locked them up.

Clayton went back out to the stage, untied Billy's horse along with the others and re-tied them to the hitching post. He then climbed aboard and prepared to leave.

"Where ya goin', boss?" Billy cried after him as he came out onto the boardwalk.

Clayton turned in the seat and smiled. "To get the preacher!"

Billy took his hat off, slapped it against his leg, and let out a holler. "Merry Christmas, boss!"

Clayton laughed as he gave a slap of the reins to get the tired horses moving. He would drive the stage to the edge of town and the preacher's house, his future bride safely tucked away beneath him in the coach. "Merry Christmas to you too, Billy!"

Christmas came with a gentle snowfall, the smell of cinnamon and pine in the air, and Clayton Riley at Summer's side. They stood in front of the preacher in the Rileys' parlor, the Christmas tree just behind him. Spencer had lit the candles on the tree one by one just before they came into the room. Summer couldn't remember ever having seen anything so beautiful.

They'd made it to the preacher's house only to find that he was at the church for the Christmas Eve service. They patiently waited for him until the service ended and folks began to make their way home before the snow got too heavy. The preacher, knowing why they were there, offered to perform the ceremony on the spot with his wife as witness. But Clayton wanted to make it extra special for Summer and asked the preacher to come out to the farm instead.

The preacher had happily agreed, but asked if his wife could come along as well. That was fine, but then Doc and Milly caught wind of what was happening and also wanted to be there. Soon the Quinns heard, and then the Johnsons, and before Clayton knew it, it was after midnight, and he had a house full of people who had dashed away from their beds and their dreams of presents and dinners to watch him get married to his mail-order bride.

Summer James, no matter what she was wearing, would have made a beautiful bride. But she was spell-binding in his mother's red dress and the hat that went with it. Mrs. Quinn gifted her with a beautiful white lace shawl that matched perfectly and seemed to glisten like the snow falling softly outside.

All was quiet and still when the wedding began, and as the Rileys had no piano in the house to play the wedding march, the townsfolk present sang instead. Instead of a wedding march to accompany Summer down the hallway from the kitchen to the parlor on Spencer's arm they sang "Silent Night." Doc and Milly started it, feeling it was fitting considering the time and date. Soft and low they sang, Mrs. Riley's soprano the most prominent among them.

Summer, despite the drama and horrors of the previous days, rejoiced that God had blessed her with a man who truly loved her. Because of her past pain and suffering she thought he'd rejected her, but he was already filling the void left behind by years of loneliness and abandonment.

She closed her eyes as she heard Clayton's firm and steady "I do." Closed them again when he kissed her, and opened them to the cheers and words of congratulations. Some folks spent the night, others traveled home with the

Johnsons to brave the snow in the morning, and Clayton, his new wife in his arms, went up to bed.

In the morning...

Spencer was the first one to come downstairs and begin to snoop under the tree for his present.

"Spencer Riley, stop that! You are not six years old!" his mother scolded.

"Aw, Ma, I at least want to see if I have anything!"

"Oh, you've got something all right, trust me!"

He smiled and took her in his arms. "You never disappoint! Whatcha make me this year? A new shirt? A scarf? I need mittens something awful, you know! Tell me you made me something to keep me warm."

Mrs. Riley winked at him.

"Mittens *and* a scarf?"

Clayton came into the parlor, Summer right behind him on her crutches. "Morning, Ma," he said, and kissed the top of her head.

"Oh, just look at you! You two look like ... like ..."

"Like they didn't get any sleep last night?" Spencer laughed.

"*Spencer* ..." Clayton warned.

Summer blushed and leaned against her new husband. No words could possibly come close to describing how she felt in that moment.

Though "at peace" covered a large portion of it.

"Let me get you two some coffee. Sit down and we'll get started opening our gifts," Mrs. Riley chirped as she headed for the kitchen.

"Gifts!" Clayton said and slapped his forehead with his hand. He turned to Summer. "I'm sorry, honey, but in all the ruckus I didn't get anything for you."

She looked up at him and smiled. "I've already had my Christmas. You've given me the best gift of all."

He kissed her then, and was still kissing her when his mother came back into the room with the coffee. Spencer made a show of looking at an invisible watch as his mother looked wide-eyed at the kissing pair.

"Ahem!" Spencer finally said.

Clayton didn't even pull away, just growled out of the corner of his mouth at his brother. "What?"

"Save it for later or I might get jealous. After all, I'm only getting a scarf and some mittens for Christmas to keep *me* warm!"

Clayton had to pull away then. He'd burst into laughter, as had Ma Riley.

"Hey, I don't think it's very funny!" Spencer blurted above the noise.

"Merry Christmas, Mrs. Riley," Summer said as Ma set the mugs on the table in front of her and Clayton.

"And Merry Christmas to you, too … *Mrs. Riley*," Ma replied.

Summer grinned and blushed.

"Well, thank you for the Christmas present,

Spence," Clayton finally said.

Spencer folded his arms across his chest and rolled his eyes. "She's non-returnable now, just so you know."

Clayton looked into Summer's smiling eyes. "I wouldn't dream of it," he whispered, then bent his head and kissed her again.

Ma Riley smiled at the kissing pair, then went to sit next to Spencer. She pulled an envelope from her apron and handed it to him. "Merry Christmas, dear."

He looked at her. "No mittens?"

She smiled and shook her head.

"I was really hoping for mittens ..."

"Open it," she urged.

Spencer opened the envelope and pulled out two pieces of paper. One was a letter written in a neat hand. The other was a ... "Good God! Mother, what have you done?"

"Now, Spencer, sometimes a mother has to take things into her own hands. After all, how can I expect you to live under the same roof with Clayton and Summer being married, and not have a wife of your own?"

Spencer stood in shock.

Summer reluctantly pulled away from the kiss, just realizing something else was happening. "What did you say?" she asked Ma Riley.

Clayton looked from his mother to Spencer and back, then burst out laughing.

"Shut up, Clayton!" Spencer cried. "This isn't funny!"

"You thought it was hilarious when you did

it to me!"

"Stop it, both of you!" their mother scolded. "Now Spencer, it's for your own good, and there's no use arguing. What's done is done!"

Summer looked from one face to the other in confusion. "What's done?"

Mrs. Riley sat up straight upon the settee and smiled. "Spencer's going to get married, dear."

"Married?" Summer asked in shock.

"Yeah, married?" Spencer added with just as much shock if not more so.

"Married, Spencer! Come on, it'll do you good!" Clayton admonished.

"But, but …"

"No buts," Mrs. Riley began. "You are getting married, Spencer, and that's final! If Clayton can have a mail-order bride and get married on Christmas then there's no reason why you can't get married on New Year's Day."

"New Year's Day! Good God, Mother, what have you *done*?"

"You asked that already, dear."

"Ma!"

Clayton stepped over to his brother and slapped him on the back. "Face it, Spence. *I'm afraid you'll just have to get hitched, and then everyone will be happy*!"

Spencer glared at his brother as he remembered saying the same words to him, the day Summer arrived in town.

"But, Spencer?" Summer asked.

"What?" Spencer groaned as he stubbornly folded his arms across his chest.

"When your bride gets to town … promise

me one thing?"

Spencer peered at her, confused. "What's that?"

It was all she could do to keep a straight face. "Try not to shoot her."

At that everyone laughed, even Spencer, who now sat on the settee and began to read the letter from his very own mail-order bride.

The End

I hope you enjoyed reading The Christmas Mail-Order Bride, the first book in the Holiday Mail-Order Bride Series. Here's a little peek at the next in the series:

THE NEW YEARS MAIL-ORDER BRIDE

ONE

New Orleans, December 1870

Elnora Barstow wasn't the most graceful thing in the world, but she wasn't a total klutz. Wouldn't you know, though, right when she needed her feet at their nimble best, they failed her.

"Run, Miss Elle!" Jethro cried as he shoved her into an alley and began to push her ahead of him at a rapid pace.

She stumbled down the alley only to trip and fall, the action toppling Jethro over like a mighty oak. He landed on the other side of her, and with lightning speed jumped to his feet. She didn't realize a man of his size could move so fast, and let out a gasp of shock when he grabbed her and pulled her up to stand before him. "We gotta move, Miss Elle! Dey be comin' round da corner any minute lookin' fo' ya!"

Elle looked up at her escort, and did her best to catch her breath. Not easy when you're frightened. "Surely we've lost them by now?"

Jethro, one of Mrs. Ridgley's two huge

Negro servants, shook his head. "No, ma'am. You don't know dis sort of men like I do. Now I gots to getcha to da train station an' on yo' way befo' dem devils finds us!"

"But Mrs. Ridgley assured me this wouldn't happen!"

"Dat was befo' dat devil-man Mr. Slade found out 'bout you! He done been snoopin' roun' da orphanage last few days, an' must've gotta look at ya somehow."

Elle's face fell. Mrs. Teeters, the head of the Winslow Orphanage, had warned her about a group of men who preyed upon the older orphan girls and tried to find when any of them were about to leave its safe confines. Having just turned eighteen a couple of weeks ago, it was time for Elle to either find decent work or a decent husband. Mrs. Teeters had strongly suggested skipping the first option, and pressed Elle to take the second: becoming a mail-order bride.

She took a deep breath. Option two was not supposed to involve running for one's life through the dark streets of New Orleans!

"Now don' be makin' no trouble for ol' Jethro, Miss Elle. We gots to be on our way!" He gave her another nudge to get her moving.

Elle was about to comment when a shot rang out. She spun at the sound, only to see Jethro, his face locked in pain, sinking to his knees. "*Run*, Miss Elle!"

She looked up. A man with a gun was standing at the other end of the alley, grinning like the devil as he made his way toward her.

"Jethro!" she gasped in panic.

Jethro clutched at the left side of his chest, his face locked in a horrible grimace as he grappled with the gun belt at his side. "Why ain't you runnin'?" he said through gritted teeth. "You gots to *run*!"

She looked at the big Negro, her heart in her throat. The bullet had passed clean through, though it must have missed his heart or he'd already be dead. She knew that much. She also knew she couldn't leave him – if she did, he'd bleed to death. But she didn't have much time.

She dropped her satchel to the ground and looked at their assailant, who had stopped twenty feet away, gun still trained on the pair. He reached into the pocket of his jacket, pulled out a crisp linen handkerchief, and casually dabbed the sweat from his brow and the back of his neck as if he had all the time in the world. Then he grinned at her once more. "Come along now, and I'll let him live," he drawled in a deep bayou accent.

She turned to Jethro, horrified. "I can't let him kill you, Jethro. I can't!"

Jethro fell forward, just catching himself with one hand. He looked up at Elle with a face so agonized it tore her heart out. "You *gots* to *go*, Miss Elle," he rasped, his voice low. "Da train ticket's in my right pocket. Take it and run. He gonna kill me no matter what. Get me my gun ..."

Elle's eyes locked on the gun belt at his side as Jethro pushed himself into a sitting position against a nearby brick wall. Blood oozed from his wound, soaking his shirt and vest.

"Whatever are you doin' talkin' with the likes o' him?" the man said casually. "Come, girl. Don't waste my time. Back away from him now."

Elle sighed as she pulled the train ticket from Jethro's vest pocket. Again she looked into his pain-filled eyes. "I'm so sorry," she whispered, and unholstered his gun for him.

"Run," Jethro rasped. "He won't shoot ya, ya ain't worth nothin' to 'im dead ..."

"I'm tired o' waitin'. Let's end this now," the man said with a sneer and began to stride toward them.

Elle saw how Jethro struggled to even reach out toward the gun in her hand ... and she didn't think, she only acted. Everything slowed until time stood still. Unthinking, she cocked the pistol, pointed it at her pursuer, squeezed the trigger ...

The shot was deafening, and she reeled back onto the hard ground. Ears ringing, she shook her own head and struggled to her knees.

Jethro sat against the wall, his head slumped to one side. "Jethro!"

He looked up at her. "Gimme dat gun, Miss Elle. Dat devil ain't gonna come after ya no mo', but ... dere might be mo' on da way ..."

Elle looked in horror at the man lying face down on the ground not feet away. "Oh my God, what have I done?" She looked desperately back to Jethro. "I killed him! Did I kill him? Oh ..."

"Gimme dat gun an' run, Miss Elle," Jethro

said weakly.

Shouts could be heard heading for the alley. "Jethro! Someone's coming!" she hissed.

"Bad men, good men, don't know which. But run, Miss Elle. Either way, I ain't goin' nowheres."

Elle dropped the pistol in his lap and began to sob.

"Go. Do it fo' me..." Jethro closed his eyes and brought the gun to his chest, where he cocked it.

The shouts drew closer.

Elle let out a final sob, grabbed her satchel, got to her feet and ran. As she fled, she prayed like she'd never prayed before – for Jethro's life, and for her own. Would they be good men or bad? How could she know? If she heard one gunshot, that meant they'd finished off the gentle giant. If there was more, maybe he survived. But if there were none, would it mean they were good men tending to him, or bad men who'd found him already dead?

She continued to flee, stumbling her way toward the train station. She wondered if she would ever know.

She finally arrived, gasping and gagging for breath, and saw the conductor hop up into a car and shout his last call of "all aboard!" The train whistle sounded, and she made one final dash with the strength she had left.

A tall, thin gentleman stood on the platform near one of the train's open doors. He glanced at Elle before looking away, then did a quick double-take.

Panic filled her as she saw his eyes narrow. She ran for the nearest car, threw her bag in and took a flying leap into it, only to bang her knee on one of the steps and go sprawling. She quickly looked over her shoulder and watched as the car moved past the man … but he gave no pursuit, as if he wasn't sure of what to do. Then, neither did she – sigh in relief, or cry at the evening's horror?

She didn't get the chance to do either, as someone yanked her to her feet. "What do you think you're doing, running after the train like that? Are you trying to get yourself killed?"

Elle looked numbly up at the conductor's scowling face. "I'm … I'm sorry, sir. I wasn't sure I was going to make it," she said between gasps.

"Are you all right?" he asked impatiently.

She nodded as she brushed off her skirt. "I think so." She checked her knee – no cut, just a bruise – then noticed he was eying her warily. "Yes, sir, I'm fine," she assured him.

He held out his hand. "Let's have a look at your ticket then."

A chill went up her spine. She looked at the ticket that was still crushed in her left hand and prayed there wasn't any blood on it – Jethro's or the other man's. Wouldn't that be tough to explain? She glanced quickly, and silently thanked the Lord when she saw it was clean of anything except her own sweat. She held it out to him. "Here you are, sir."

The conductor took it from her, read it and whistled. "Salt Lake City, eh? Long way to go –

end of the line, in fact. Just where are you heading, miss?"

Elle finally let herself relax as she retrieved her satchel. "Nowhere, sir."

Nowhere, Washington Territory, New Year's Day 1871

"Spencer? Spencer! It's time to go – do hurry, dear!" Leona Riley called up the stairs. She stood in front of a mirror that hung in the front hall and adjusted her hat, then pulled on her gloves. "Where is that boy?" she remarked to herself.

"I'm coming, Ma!" Spencer Riley said as he stomped down the stairs to where she stood. "The stage isn't gonna be here for an hour. We have plenty of time ..."

"I know, but you can't be too careful," she replied as she inspected him. "Is that shirt clean?"

"For heaven's sake, Ma, I'm not ten years old! Of course my shirt is clean! My shoes are shined, my socks don't have any holes. I even polished the bullets in my revolver, if you must know."

Mrs. Riley's mouth opened in shock. "You did *what*?"

Spencer chuckled. "I'm kidding, Ma. Now let's go."

Mrs. Riley eyed her younger son and

smirked. He was nervous, she could tell. She hoped she'd made the right decision when she took matters into her own hands a few months ago and came up with the brilliant idea of sending away for a mail-order bride for her elder son Clayton. Spencer had been all for it at the time, and played an integral part in pulling the whole thing off while keeping his big brother none the wiser. What Spencer hadn't known was that, not a week later, she'd sent away for *another* mail-order bride – this time for Spencer himself.

She'd delivered the news to him Christmas Day as his present – an envelope with a letter from his future bride and a marriage contract written up by The Ridgley Mail-Order Bride Service of New Orleans, Louisiana. He was shocked at what she'd done, but soon adjusted to the idea. He'd had no choice – his bride had already taken the train from New Orleans to Salt Lake, preparing to board a stage the day after Christmas to finish out the remainder of the journey.

She was arriving today, and Spencer was beside himself with worry. All he had was a letter from the girl, no picture. Likewise, she had no picture of him – only a small note written by his mother.

"How could you have done such a thing?" he'd lamented to his mother all through Christmas Day.

"Now, Spencer, it's for your own good! And besides, I'm sure she'll be beautiful! Just look at what a beautiful bride that Mrs. Ridgley sent

Clayton! I'm sure she'll send you someone equally as pretty."

Spencer had still moaned and groaned over the prospect. And it hadn't taken long for the rest of Nowhere to catch wind of what was going on. Soon the whole town, already primed by Clayton's marriage, was abuzz with the news of another upcoming wedding.

Of course, many a pretty miss was crushed by the news. For years, Spencer had been considered the catch of Nowhere, but no one had caught his eye. Charlotte Davis had tried for as long as anyone could remember to nail Clayton down – before he'd married Sarah, and after her untimely death – and when he was wed she'd taken a run at Spencer, to his massive disinterest. Folks were speculating whether or not she'd have another go at Spencer now that Clayton was spoken for, but so far she'd given no indication of it.

Just as well, Spencer thought. He had enough to fret about. On top of his mother surprising him with a mail-order bride for New Year's instead of the new scarf and mittens he'd wanted (the usual tradition in the Riley household), Clayton had informed him he was stepping down as the town sheriff – and naming Spencer to replace him!

Spencer pinned the silver star to his vest, put on his coat and hat, then turned to his mother. "All right, let's go. But I still don't know if this is a good idea."

"Oh, Spencer – you'll love her, I'm sure! Just as Clayton loves Summer."

"I don't even know what she looks like."

"It didn't stop your brother." Mrs. Riley knew that would get a rise out of him – what younger sibling wants to be compared to the older one? "And she doesn't know what you look like either!"

"If we don't suit, I'm sending her back …"

"Clayton said the same thing. And she's still here, and your sister-in-law besides."

"But Summer is beautiful, both inside and out. I wouldn't have sent her back either!"

"But your brother is less agreeable than you are. It's a good thing he shot her when he did."

"Ma, don't say that! It's *not* a good thing he shot her at all!"

"Oh, stop fussing – I know it was an accident! But it did keep Summer around long enough for them to fall in love."

"Well, I think I'll keep my gun in its holster, thank you!" Spencer admonished as he helped his mother up into the wagon.

She eyed him as she took her seat and he hopped up next to her. "Of course you are, son. You'll just have to fall in love with her the good old-fashioned way. It'll take the time it takes."

Spencer gave the horses a good slap with the reins. "Ma, when are you going to stop romanticizing everything? What if love *doesn't* come in time? I'd like to at least get to know her first before I marry her." He suddenly looked at his mother, his brow furrowed. "You didn't make arrangements with the preacher for a wedding right away, I hope."

His mother suddenly became interested in the

snow-covered landscape as they pulled out of the barnyard. "I do hope my asters come up well this spring."

"Mother," Spencer said in warning. "What have you done?"

"Well, you know that by the time the stage pulls into town, church services will be getting out."

Spencer pulled back on the reins and brought the wagon to a halt. "I am not getting married to someone right after they get off the stage! I have my limits, Mother!"

"Why not, dear? Other men do."

"Other men at least get to exchange letters with their intended before finally meeting them. I have *one* letter, in response to a note *you* wrote!"

"Her name is Miss Barstow, dear."

"I'm aware," he replied in frustration. "For another thing, *you* picked her out!"

"Actually, Mrs. Ridgley picked her out. But I have complete trust in her judgment." She crossed her arms over her chest. "Did you share any of this with Clayton? I know he hasn't been around much this last week, what with him retiring and you taking over the office."

"No, I hadn't thought about it up until now. Clayton's been too busy during the day … and just as busy at night."

His mother gasped. "Spencer!"

"Well, he *is* married now, Ma. What do you expect? Don't you want grandchildren?"

"Of course I do, but you don't have to talk about the details."

"You're the one that brought it up."

And on it went for the rest of their trip into town. Spencer loved his mother, loved her with all his heart, but to be honest, Leona Riley could be a trial at times. In a loving, motherly, I'm-going-to-do-what-I-think-is-best-for-you sort of way, but still a trial. This was definitely one of those times.

He'd tried to push the whole ordeal out of his mind the first few days by busying himself with making a list of his new duties as sheriff. Clayton wanted to get back to apple farming, and Spencer was all for it. He was also the logical choice to take Clayton's place.

But realizing why Clayton wanted to farm again – so he could be near his wife to keep her safe and sound – made Spencer wonder if he was doing the right thing. After all, if he got married, wouldn't he want to do the same thing? Then again, if his new wife turned out to be undesirable, maybe he would want to be away from home, taking advantage of a sheriff's long hours ...

He'd gone over it and over it in his mind for the last week: what he would do if he found his new bride to be less than he hoped for. What if she was a quiet, demure little thing that did whatever he asked? Would he be happy with that? What if she was cantankerous and argued a lot? Would he be able to show her what was what and who was boss in his house? What if he thought she was ugly as a troll and couldn't bear to share his bed? Even worse, what if *she* turned out to be beautiful beyond compare, but thought *he* was ugly as a troll and *wouldn't* share his bed?

He shuddered at the thought as he pulled into town, parked the wagon, set the brake and hopped to the frozen ground. He went around the wagon to help his mother climb down, and they went across the street to the sheriff's office.

Clayton was standing outside, and he shook Spencer's hand as his brother stepped up onto the boardwalk. "Are you ready for this?" he asked in a low tone.

Spencer took a deep breath. "As ready as I'll ever be."

Clayton let go a chuckle. "She'll be beautiful, you'll see."

"What if she's not? What if she's cranky and looks like a Guernsey?"

Clayton looked him right in the eye. "You can always send her back."

Then they heard it – the stage. "Oh, here it comes!" their mother cried.

The stage rolled into town and approached them at a good pace. The lead driver waved his hat at them as he pulled back on the reins and brought the team to a stop just past the sheriff's office. Spencer, Clayton, and their mother walked down the boardwalk as one of the drivers jumped down and went to open the door so the passengers could disembark.

Spencer stopped short and turned to his brother. "What am I doing? How could I have let Ma talk me into this?"

"This isn't the time for cold feet, Spence."

"But what if she hates me? What if I can't

stand *her*?"

"Spencer …" Clayton groaned.

"What if she's covered in warts and hates little children?"

"Oh, for crying out loud!"

"What if she has a hidden past? What if she's *really* running from the law? Remember how you thought Summer might be?"

"Spencer!"

"What if …"

He never got to finish. Clayton grabbed him and spun him around to face the young woman just getting off the stage. "And what if that's her, you fall in love, and live happily ever after?" he hissed.

Spencer's mouth dropped open as he shook his head. "Things don't happen that way, but I suppose I could give it a try."

The woman looked up at him, her eyes wide, and mumbled something to herself before she said, "Excuse me, sir. I'm looking for a Spencer Riley. Do any of you know where I might find him?"

Spencer stood there, stunned into silence. This … this vision of loveliness was *her*?

Clayton rolled his eyes and gave his brother a nudge with his elbow.

Shaken out of his stupor, Spencer stepped forward. "Um … I'm Spencer Riley, ma'am."

She took a deep breath, smiled nervously and said, "Hello, Mr. Riley. I'm Elnora Barstow – your mail-order bride?"

ABOUT THE AUTHOR

Kit Morgan, aka Geralyn Beauchamp loves a good Western. Her father loved them as well, and they watched their fair share together over the years. To find out about upcoming releases and other fun news about Kit Morgan's books, sign up for her newsletter at her website: **www.authorkitmorgan.com**